LOST DIARIES

VOLUME ONE

STILL HUMAN

JEPH PORTER

MAPLIGHT
PRESS
www.maplightpress.com

BIG DEAL

Max knew he'd be able to find what he needed at the Big Deal. The store was iconic, the big blue letters hanging on the giant building the size of a warehouse were as recognizable as Coca-Cola or Walt Disney. Every American knew that if they needed anything at all, they were in luck because every small town or mid-sized city had a Big Deal ready to sell them whatever they desired. Max, however, had not been in a Big Deal in years. A schism existed between the city folk and the country folk in the matter of public judgment on Big Deals, and Max sat firmly on one side of the divide. Ever since he left his hometown of Jackson, Illinois, for Chicago, he had avoided the metastatic big-box store as a rule and a mandate of his self-prescribed moral superiority—unless he really had no other choice, of course. The last time he could recall being inside a Big Deal was when he was back in Jackson, and that had been over a decade ago.

What had forced his hand today was lack of choice. This was the secret to Big Deal's success, of course. They had strangled out any other shops and if you happened to find yourself on a road trip, as Max was with his wife Jessica, and you needed something, there was always a Big Deal right off the highway that would be happy to help. On this day, Max and Jessica had been on their way to Indiana to enjoy a weekend at the Dunes, and Max had forgotten a memory card for his brand-new camera. Photography had always been a hobby of his, something he picked up from his father, and he was looking forward to capturing proof that Indiana had picturesque locations.

He promised Jessica that he wouldn't be long and left her waiting patiently in the car with the air conditioner still running and Fleetwood Mac on the stereo and jogged across the parking lot, dodging cars and shoppers with heavy carts barely under their control towards one of the two giant entrances on either side of the massive building. Even though he had never been in this particular Big Deal, he knew, without even consulting a map of the store, where to find what he came for. In an unsettling way, the familiarity was soothing. But when he stepped through the sliding glass doors he had a dizzying sense of deja vu. Had he actually been to this one before? As far as he could tell, this layout was exactly the same as the layout of the Big Deal in his hometown. This realization triggered an involuntary wave of dread. It had been a long time since he'd been to his hometown, but really, not long enough.

Like all Big Deals, there was a full grocery store on one side with all the food and food-related items you could ever want and on the other side a store that had everything else you could ever want. Max had entered on the grocery side and he knew that if he walked down the large aisle in front of him, he would come to another main thoroughfare that ran past the shoe section, the back side of the home goods section, and then finally to the electronics department where he would find a camera section.

This small aisle of cameras brought back memories of waiting in line to collect the photos he'd taken on the disposable cameras his father would often give him. He recalled the joy of peeling open that little paper folder stuffed with his prints and thumbing through them like they were Italian masterpieces on four-by-six glossy photo paper.

His father had been a photographer for The Jackson Herald. When one of his photos would make the front page, Max would proudly point it out to his friends. It, too, a masterpiece.

His father was there the day the category four tornado leveled Teasdale Court, a suburb on the northwest side of town, even before the big national news organizations got there. That week his photos had been shown on the national news and even The New York Times. Max had a special place in his mind for memories like that. The good ones. He had an entire second location up there for the others. And he never liked to access either of them because one always led to the other, and the cascade of memories would end like it was now: him looking at the camera accessories in the back of the Big Deal, trying not to think about why he didn't speak to his father anymore.

His brain was able to scan the little hanging placards of memory cards while, at the same time, thinking about how much of a bitter and entitled man his father had become after Max's mother died. He could feel his cheeks getting hot as he remembered how he felt when the one person he wanted to grieve with seemed incapable of doing anything but making it about himself. And without the one person they needed to bring them together, they drifted apart, unable to find a way back to each other.

Max grabbed a thirty-two-gigabyte memory card and turned out of the aisle as quickly as possible. Thankfully the "big" in Big Deal came to his rescue as there were about a dozen open checkout stations. Max rushed for the self-checkout, swiped his item, and tapped his card to pay. He was walking towards the exit in less than three minutes.

The sliding doors pushed open, letting in a blast of the

afternoon heat and Max squinted at the sunlight bouncing off the roofs of the cars. He had decided to use the store side exit nearest the self-checkouts rather than the one he had entered, but he realized he would have to walk further across the sun-baked asphalt.

He wasn't going back in that store, though, so he moved across the parking lot and as his eyes adjusted to the light he stopped short suddenly unsure where he had parked. He looked for any familiar landmarks and strangely, he found many but they were not the same he remembered seeing when they drove in. At the far edge, near the highway, he saw a row of fast food restaurants. Burger King, Carl's Jr., and a Mindy's Pizza? Those had not been there before. In fact, Mindy's Pizza was a regional chain he remembered from growing up. They had one right outside the Big Deal in Jackson. As he looked around some more, a profound sense of confusion overtook him. The rest of the landmarks looked identical to the ones outside the Big Deal in Jackson. A used sporting goods store, a cell phone shop, and a Mexican restaurant called El Dorado that everyone in Jackson pronounced "El De-RAY-dough".

His stomach sank and he felt that sense of dread again. It was impossible, but he seemed to be standing in the parking lot of the Big Deal in Jackson, Illinois, a place he hadn't been in over a decade.

He turned back to look at the store and saw the same familiar doors from all those years ago and also just ten minutes ago. He might have stood there staring for a very long time if a large red truck with giant black wheels propping it four feet off the ground hadn't roared its horn. Max looked up to see a very annoyed woman throwing her hands up like he was the world's biggest idiot. He quickly walked back towards the store and stood out front for a long moment, completely unsure what to do. Finally he reached for his phone, but realized he had left it in the car with Jessica so she could keep listening to the road trip playlist.

Max wandered back inside the store and took a long, slow look around from the entrance. There was a line of checkout stations to his left stretching all the way back to the grocery section. There was a Subway sandwich shop on that end as well, and the bakery and the grocery section past that. To his right was the pharmacy and the massive women's department was ahead of him. This was the same store he had just been in, but it was also the same store from his memory. A man in a blue vest approached and asked if there was anything he could help him with.

"No," Max said with a smile, but then stopped the man and asked if there was a phone he could use. The man thought about it for a moment and then decided that Max looked non-threatening enough that he would allow it.

He followed the man to the customer service desk, which was halfway down the long row of checkouts, past the in-house vision clinic, and the portrait studio which Max was surprised still existed. When he arrived at the customer service desk, the man in the blue vest put in a good word for him to a woman in a gray vest, which seemed to indicate that she was a higher-ranking officer than him.

She nodded. "What number do you want to dial, hun?"

He thought about it and had a second horrifying realization that he didn't know his wife's phone number. He wasn't even sure of the area code. The only number he still had memorized was the home phone number of his parents' house, which had long been disconnected. Many times he had dialed that number after soccer practice at school or when he was ready to be picked up from a friend's after an afternoon of hanging out. It was the only time he got to hear her speak to him like she would speak to any other adult. Until she would realize it was him and drop all the formality that went away with someone you were so close to. In a panic Max blurted the number out and the woman dialed it on the desk phone before handing him the receiver. After a few rings, a woman answered.

"Hello?" she said in a soft, formal tone and Max almost collapsed there at the desk.

He was talking to his dead mother.

<hr>

The man in the blue vest, who had been going above and beyond today, gave Max a little cup of water as he sat on a bench just outside the portrait studio. He hadn't managed to say a single word to the woman on the phone before he fell to the floor. The gray-vested woman had briefly apologized to the caller and hung up as the blue-vested man lifted Max to his feet and guided him to the bench, where he now sat. The man asked if there was anything else he could help him with and Max said no, he didn't know what to do. He didn't feel up to trying anymore phone numbers, even his own, and getting anymore surprises. He wanted to find Jessica and get the hell out of there. After a moment he could tell the man was ready to stop attending to him, so Max thanked him and moved towards the exit closest to the self checkouts.

He found himself in the parking lot again, same fast food restaurants, and the same strip of stores running along the west side of the parking lot. He tried to look for his car, but after he walked the grid of the parking lot twice over, he couldn't find it. Had Jessica been looking for him? Maybe she had decided to leave? This thought struck him as ridiculous though because why would she be looking for him in a town that was five hours south of where he had left her? Surely she'd tried to call and realized his phone was in the car. But would she go in the store looking for him? Would she, too, suddenly appear hundreds of miles away in his hometown? The blue-vested man eyed him from the front of the store, clearly considering if he needed to call the police. So Max headed for the intersection by the highway that was vaguely in the direction of downtown.

Jackson wasn't a walking city, at least not this far out. There wasn't even a sidewalk for ninety percent of the walk down Lake Street, the main road across town. He thought about breaking off and walking down some quieter streets to avoid the traffic and the sun, but he had a sense that he should stay on the main roads just in case he wasn't as confident about the geography of Jackson as he recalled. Maybe this was all some mad dream and he was currently being rushed out of the electronics aisle on a gurney with drool rolling out of his mouth. Strangely he hoped so. It sounded better than trudging along the uneven grass toward downtown Jackson as cars sped by, spitting up dust and debris. There was nothing for him to actually do once he got downtown and no one for him to find and ask for help. The only person he knew that still lived in Jackson was his dad and he wasn't about to bring him into this situation.

Then he remembered JB.

He had gone to high school with JB and while they weren't best friends he had maintained a form of contact with him. He would hear from him from time to time mostly via texts but the last he heard, JB still lived in Jackson. His mother had died years ago and left him the family home which, if his sense of direction was correct, was not far from where he was standing now.

He hurried across the huge intersection and onto the grass lawn of the First Christian Disciples church. Past the church, he finally turned off the main road and down the slowly winding neighborhood drive. Not only was the traffic much lighter, but there was a decent amount of shade as well. As he recalled, JB's house was just at the end of the first cul-de-sac. He'd never really taken the time to see any of the other houses in this small neighborhood. Their siding was fading and in some places falling off. In his memory, or the scattered images of it anyway, Max had assumed these were nicer homes. Something about the curve of the road and big shady trees suggested wealth to him. Maybe there had been wealth here once, or the promise of it anyway. These homes were built in a time when a middle class family could easily acquire a five-bedroom home with a large yard, but those days had faded away.

When Max made it to the cul-de-sac, he saw two cars parked in JB's drive. A purple minivan and a black four-door coupe that looked like it belonged in a scrap yard. Max knocked on the front door and felt his breath coming in short bursts. He had planned a weekend of hiking but he realized he might not be equipped for it.

An older woman in her 60s appeared, barely visible behind the screen door. Max explained who he was in as casual a tone as he could muster and asked if JB was home. The woman nodded and called for him without inviting the strange sweaty man inside.

After an agonizing few minutes, JB lumbered up to the door. Max didn't really know how he expected JB to react to this sudden appearance on his front porch but it wasn't by standing there for a very long time saying nothing. Sure, it was weird he was here unannounced, but a visit wasn't entirely out of the realm of possibility.

"Hey JB," Max waved at him, trying to act like this was all perfectly normal. "Long time no see."

JB stood silently looking at him and Max sensed that his concern at seeing him wasn't just temporary confusion. JB was very freaked out.

Finally he pushed open the screen door and waved him inside. Max followed him down a set of stairs to his bedroom. The piles of clothes and fast food take-out wrappers might have embarrassed anyone else with an unexpected guest but JB threw a cautious glance upstairs and then whispered urgently.

"You went in the Big Deal, didn't you?"

"Yeah, why?" Max asked cautiously. He was curious to know why JB knew that.

"That's how you got here," he explained.

"Where is here?" Max asked as JB led him to a couch on one side of the room and sat him down.

"We're in an alternate dimension, dude."

Max tried to process this. His mind fought, of course. It told him that this was impossible and that what had really happened was that he was suffering from some severe memory loss and he had somehow made it down to Jackson without knowing it. Or maybe this was all some incredible dream?

"It's not a dream, you're not crazy, and no, you haven't been in some freak accident." JB assured him. "You went into a Big Deal wherever you were and you came out in Jackson. It happens all the time."

"All the time?"

"Enough that I know about it."

"How come this hasn't happened to me before?"

"When's the last time you were in a Big Deal?"

Max took his point even if it didn't answer anything.

"I don't understand," Max said. "Does this happen to everyone?"

"Only people from Jackson."

"Well how come I've never heard of it?"

"Because anyone that moves away never goes into a Big Deal, so they never get transported back by walking out of the wrong door!"

"The wrong door?"

JB looked at him, realizing that Max still had no clue what he had stumbled into.

"You went in on the grocery side and exited on the store side. That's how it works."

"What do you mean 'that's how it works?'" Max was losing patience with JB's annoyance at him for not grasping this cosmic concept. "How do you know?"

"Because that's how I got here!" JB shouted and then threw a concerned look towards the stairs.

"But why are you here?" Max asked, lowering his voice.

"Accident at first," JB said, matching Max's tone and turning away from him. "Honestly, most people in Jackson use the same exit and don't jump dimensions. Those who don't, don't seem to notice, I guess, but I did." JB looked at the stairs again. "I started coming back on purpose because, well, Ma' is dead in the other world but she's not here."

Max looked up towards the stairs and realized that the old woman who had answered the door was JB's mom. He had known her when they were in high school but she had died pretty shortly after he met JB. He didn't recognize her not just because she was hidden by the screen door, but because she had aged like anyone would that hadn't died.

JB had reached out to Max when his own mother died and they had a few drinks after the funeral. But neither of them knew how to comfort the other even if they wanted to. If it was even possible. Had JB known about this place all along?

"Wait. I talked to my mom on the phone," Max realized. "Is she alive here too?"

JB looked at him for a long moment, then shrugged.

"Maybe. Weird things happen here."

"Is this like a universe where moms don't die?"

"No. It's a parallel universe. Lots of things are different. The mom thing is just a coincidence."

Max thought about the possibility of this being a coincidence and it seemed like an almost too improbable thing in an already improbable day.

"That's weird," he said out loud.

"*That's* weird? *That's* weird?!" JB exploded. But he still managed to keep his voice low. "You've just traveled through time and space via a freaking big-box store and the fact that both our moms are alive is the weird part?!"

Max apologized for offending him and quickly asked how he could get back. His thoughts went to Jessica, probably still sitting in the air-conditioned car. Had she called the police yet? Had she thought the worst yet?

"You just go back inside and exit through the other exit," JB explained like it was the simplest thing in the world.

"But I went back inside -" Max started to explain.

"You've got to exit through the other exit!" JB cut him off, already annoyed again at having to repeat himself. "If you go through the same exit you entered, you don't go anywhere. If you use a different exit from the one you entered, you end up here."

Max looked at him for a long moment.

"Come on. I'll give you a ride," JB said and moved towards the stairs.

"So you live here and in the other world?" Max asked, not moving from his spot on the couch. JB stopped at the first stair and looked at Max like he was ready for these questions. "What about your other self?" Max asked.

"We have an arrangement," was all JB would offer.

"That doesn't cause like, a paradox?"

"It's not time-travel, dude. It's dimension hopping. You can't create a paradox. You're in two separate universes."

JB leveled a curious glance at him as he saw Max working out the details in his head. "But you can't go fucking around with people's lives." He waved a dismissive hand in front of him as if this would wash away the machinations forming in Max's mind. "It's the same way it is in the other place. It's not consequence free." Max considered this.

"Can we make a stop before we go back?"

JB's car pulled up at the corner of Dennis St. and Fallon Ave. in the city's historic West End neighborhood. Max looked out the window at the very familiar oak tree at the edge of the big yard. This was the home he had grown up in. His room was on the second floor overlooking the street. He had parked his first car in the very spot they were now sitting in.

"This is a very classic, bad idea." JB said, looking at him from the driver's seat.

"I'm going to be okay," Max assured him.

"Alright well, make it quick," JB said shifting in his seat. "I've got dinner plans."

Max crawled out of the car and walked across the lawn to the front door of the historic home. His hands were shaking again and he felt like he might pass out but he steadied himself on the banister and knocked. After a long moment his mother came to the door, looking confused. She half smiled at him and Max could feel his head spinning and the tears coming. She opened the door, her face now concerned, and he fell into her arms crying.

His mother led him inside and into the dining room. The table was the same table they had had when he was growing up, but things like that seemed to finally make sense. It would be stranger if it wasn't, he thought.

"I didn't know you were in town," his mother said timidly and he sensed there was some tension there. Perhaps the odd look and her acceptance of him breaking down into tears was not a result of her clear understanding of the situation.

"Jessica and I, we, we were on a trip..." he began but then didn't know how to explain.

"Who's Jessica?"

Of course she wouldn't know. She died before he had met

Jessica. But then again, here she was. He realized she was projecting her knowledge of him from this world onto him. A version of him that also hadn't visited in a while.

"She's my wife."

His mother's eyes went wide and he could see the flush in her cheeks. Why hadn't he invited her to the wedding? He felt sad and confused all at once. And then he was angry, why hadn't he, the him in this dimension, invited her to the wedding? Was he even married here? Did he even know Jessica in this world?

"You come all the way from California with no notice and tell me you're married?" his mother fumed.

"No, Mom, please, let's sit down and talk."

She looked at him and saw the seriousness in his eyes. Reluctantly she took a seat and waited for him to explain this injustice.

"I don't live in California," he began.

"And you've moved? You didn't think to tell me?"

"I've never lived in California. I'm not from here," he said slowly. His mother waited for him to unwind this puzzle for her. "This is almost impossible to believe but I'm from another dimension. A dimension in which—" he felt his throat tighten as the enormity of it all hit him. "A dimension in which...you're dead."

"I'm calling the police," she stood from the table.

"No, Mom, listen to me. I'm not joking."

"I know you're not joking," she said and stood up to move towards the kitchen. "You've finally had a mental break and you're here to get revenge on me for killing your father."

"What?!" Max was pinned to his chair. The bark-like utterance stopped his mother also. She looked at him with deep realization.

"Your father, Max," she said slowly. "He died years ago in the accident. I was driving the car and you never forgave me."

Max felt himself melting now. His body shook and all he

could do was put his head on the table. His mother, seeing her son in a state of abject devastation, moved over to him, and despite her anger, put her hand on his back.

"Max, are you okay?"

He didn't answer for a long time. He might not have been able to pull himself out of the hole of shame and anger he felt for never fixing his relationship with his father if he hadn't remembered the absurdity of his situation. His father wasn't dead. His mother was dead. But now she was alive. His father was also alive.

"He's alive!" Max popped up from the chair startling his mother.

"I think you should calm down, Max."

"No, I'm fine Mom. Listen, Dad is alive. In my dimension, he's alive."

"Max, honey, I'm going to call someone."

"No, no," Max pleaded. "Let me show you."

"Show me what?"

"My dimension."

She looked at him for a long moment. Her eyes scanned his face and despite the smile that was still wet with his tears or maybe because of it, she knew he was not lying.

"He's alive?" She asked and Max nodded. "And you can show me him?" Max nodded and took her hand.

"Come with me," Max said and made a move for the front door but his mother didn't follow.

"Come on, we have to go to the Big Deal," Max said, beckoning her to follow him.

"The Big Deal?" she spat out, her concern for her son suddenly escalating again.

"Yeah, there is a portal there. JB told me about it. You remember JB? From high school? He's here. He can take us." Max was practically bouncing now. He had his hand on the door knob but his mother hadn't moved from the dining room.

"I'm not going anywhere with JB."

Max realized the enormity of the ask. The great mental burden one would have to take on to believe one word of what he was excited about. He let go of the door and tried to think of how he could convince her.

"I'll meet you there," she said before he could even try, already reaching for her purse on the table.

Max smiled and opened the door.

JB was not happy about the plan Max had devised. He yelled at him about it the whole way to the Big Deal.

"If you and I can go back and forth freely, why can't she?" Max argued.

"It's not about the back and forth," JB said, "It's about the ramifications of bringing your father and mother back together. You don't think that's going to mess things up?"

"My life has been pretty messed up since the day of that accident. I don't see how this could make things worse."

JB gave him a look that seemed to say, "Yeah that's the problem." But he didn't vocalize it.

They got to the store and Max bounded out of the car looking for his mother. JB sat in his car and refused to get out. Max assured him it was okay.

"You're an expert now?" he huffed. "I don't want to be around to see whatever cosmic shit you unleash."

Max thanked him for all of his help and with a reluctant nod and a wave, JB drove the half-junk coupe out of the parking lot.

Max waited by the store side entrance for a while. After almost an hour he started to believe she wasn't coming. Of course she wasn't. Why would she? Whoever he was in this universe was clearly unwell and his ravings about a dimensional portal in the Big Deal only confirmed that.

He thought about walking back to try and convince her but would it be worth it? Was it a good idea to stay here any longer? Jessica had probably reported him missing by now and he expected to find flashing red and blue lights when he crossed back over. They'd take him away when he tried to explain where he was. But if he had his mother with him, then they'd have to believe him. She had to come.

Finally, he saw a car pull into the parking lot near El Dorado. His mother got out slowly and made her way to him.

"Ready?" he asked her as she approached and she nodded. He reached for her hand and they walked into the store side entrance. They walked past the vision clinic, the portrait studio, the line of checkouts, and finally the Subway. Max tried to notice any kind of cosmic shift in space time that might occur as they neared the other entrance but he felt nothing. His mother hurried behind him as he pulled her along, her eyes darting around nervously as they passed the customer service desk where the gray-vested woman took no notice.

Finally they approached the sliding doors of the second entrance and Max barreled through it pulling them both into the slightly chillier northern Indiana day. His eyes blinked and he saw the parking lot full of cars and this time, no fast food restaurants, no used sporting goods store, and no El Dorado. His mother pulled her hand out of his and stopped.

"Come on," Max said. "Jessica is right over here. We'll get in the car and go find Dad."

His mother didn't say anything. Her eyes surveyed the area taking it all in. She bit her lip and squeezed her arms tight around her body as she confirmed that what she was seeing was real.

"Come on," Max reached for her hand, but she wouldn't let him take it. She shook her head and took a few steps back toward the door. "Mom, come on. We can go find Dad right now."

She shook her head again. "No, Max," she said. "I'm not going."

"What are you talking about? Don't you want to see Dad?"

"No," she said, "I miss him everyday but I buried him years ago. I only came with you to make sure you weren't—to make sure you were okay."

Max reached for her again.

"But Dad's not dead. He's alive."

"For you he is."

Max's hand hung in the air and he realized that he had been spending so much time missing his mother that he hadn't realized how much time he was missing with his father. Here was a woman who had lost her husband and had made peace with that. Why hadn't he?

"I'm going back, Max," she said. "I'm going to call my son."

"Mom," Max said half pleading.

"I love you, Max," she said.

Max stepped forward and pulled her into a hug. She squeezed him back and then clawed herself away from him. She wiped a few tears from her own eyes and then darted back into the store. Max watched her go and he would have stood there forever if there wasn't a loud piercing honk from a black BMW that had been waiting for him to get out of the road.

He looked around and saw no flashing lights or teams of police combing the area for him. He just saw one angry driver giving him the finger. He shuffled across the parking lot and found their Prius idling with the soft tones of Stevie Nicks filtering through the doors. How long had he been gone? It was hours on the other side, but there was no way Jessica would have sat here that long without freaking out. But when he climbed into the driver's seat, he found her asleep. The sound of the car door opening roused her, and she looked around confused.

"Sorry, it's just me," Max said.

She asked him if he found what he needed. He stared out the window at the sliding doors that led back into the Big Deal and back to his hometown.

"Yeah, I did."

THE DAY OF THE STRANGE

I PAUSED THE VIDEO ON MY PHONE, FREEZING THE pale, redheaded girl mid-bounce, her mouth caught in an "O." Just a few minutes ago she had been all I wanted in the world, the missing puzzle piece to the—who the hell knows? But now that I was... finished, all I could think was: Who was she? Did she actually enjoy this? What happened in her life that got her here? Why did humans need things like this to exist? Was it good for us? Was it something we should be ashamed of? What happened to my life that I was here alone and asking myself existential questions about a video on the internet called *Starr Rogan Tricks Coach Into After School Lesson*.

I let my phone drop to the floor and flipped the light off. Another day over, and another night capped off with a meaningless shot in the dark.

I forgot to set my alarm and woke up too late to catch the 7am bus. That meant I'd have to catch the next one. "Fuck it," I thought. I was already late, so I might as well take another few minutes to get some more sleep. I told myself just five more minutes and I'd feel so much better. I'd get that project done at work that was already a week late and my boss would be so happy he'd forget I walked in the door over an hour after I was supposed to. Hell, I'd make it up to him and be on time every day this week.

I rolled over and wound my arms around a woman lying on her side next to me in bed. She was naked and pale. There were zits on her back and she smelled like strawberry soda.

My heart jumped into my throat and I leapt out of bed. The woman stirred and looked at me. She yawned, stretching her arms, revealing her naked chest with no inhibition. Her red hair was tousled and heavy-blue eyeshadow and red lipstick were painted on her like she was a billboard for a clown college.

"Who—who—who..." I stuttered, laughing as if this was my fault, as if I'd forgotten something. Did I go out last night? Did someone come over? I didn't recall either of these scenarios yet somehow there was a woman in my bed.

She smiled, coiled her arms around her chest, and nestled her head on the pillow.

"Come back to bed," she cooed through parted lips, the glint of her tongue ring just visible, and patted the now empty spot where I had been lying.

As I ran through the events of the previous evening over and over again in my head, the only thing that I could connect to this redheaded, face-painted, pale, naked woman lying in my bed was the phrase: "Starr Rogan Tricks Coach Into After School Lesson."

What did that mean!?

It hit me like the first drop of a roller coaster. I looked at this woman in my bed who couldn't be older than twenty, and despite the absurdity of it, I realized she was the very same girl I was watching through my phone screen last night. Except here she was, not images and progress bars but flesh, and presumably all of the same fluids.

"You're..." I couldn't say it.

She closed her eyes and pouted her lips.

"You're..." I tried again.

"So horny," she answered coyly.

"I have to go to work," I said, darting out of the room.

My redheaded friend walked a pace behind me on the sidewalk. I couldn't stop her; she just got dressed, in the same lime-green barely-there one-piece she was wearing in the video, and followed me out. I tried to lose her by weaving in and out of people on the sidewalk, but she was unsurprisingly nimble. I wasn't the only one walking around with a scantily-clad visitor by my side. Mr. Jurkowski, the corner store owner, stood with a six-foot-tall woman in a leopard print dress and platform silver high heels with laces wrapped up to her knees. Mr. Jurkowski was watering the plants out front and she was moisturizing a peach with her tongue. Mr. Jurkowski was trying his best to ignore her, but she was doing her work just a few inches from his face. I asked myself if this woman had always worked for Mr. Jurkowski or was he actually suffering the same plight as me? When the woman switched from fellating the peach to licking Mr. Jurkowski's cheek, I had my answer.

The city bus was crowded; the school year had just started and seemingly every high school student in the city was packed onto this public bus, some sitting sheepishly next to porn stars I unfortunately recognized, what were probably influencers, and more disturbingly, a few duplicates of their classmates. The last one I might not have noticed if I hadn't seen at the other end of the bus a few of the original versions, their faces, flush with embarrassment, hung toward the ground.

Starr did her best to make the bus ride uncomfortable for

me as well. Her eager hands kept exploring my inseam no matter how many times I batted them away. Her playful laughing drew looks of sympathy from the other riders who were dealing with similar problems. But no one maintained eye contact too long in a vain hope that no one would notice something that everyone was noticing.

After the excruciating bus ride, I ran across the parking lot to my office building, my redheaded stalker clacking her high heels on the pavement in pursuit, and saw several coworkers also arriving late and walking quickly, with someone in pursuit.

"You can't come in here," I told Starr sternly as I tried to hold the door. But a woman I recognized from the cafeteria pulled open the door next to it as she ran away from a tall Brazilian man in a loose silk shirt, and Starr slipped in behind her. "I can't swipe you in," I said apologetically, showing her my key card. But when I looked at Carl, the security guard, for confirmation, I saw he was dealing with his own incursion into his privacy in the form of a generously proportioned woman that he looked at skeptically, but not entirely disdainfully, and he waved us through the gate.

I opened the fridge in the breakroom and stuffed my lunch in the back. My redheaded other half was eying the vending machine. I wondered if she was hungry.

"Do you need to... eat?" I asked, unsure.

"MmmHmm." She nodded. "I'm hungry for *you*, baby."

"Oh, well," I said. "I've got a meeting first thing here, so maybe after?" But she wasn't paying attention. She was gyrating and humping on the glass of the vending machine causing the Gardetto's to rattle in their bags.

The meeting wasn't awkward at all. My boss, Jerry, glanced around the conference room nervously as he tried to ignore the large Hispanic woman cleaning the table in front of him. At first I thought she might be a member of the cleaning staff, but her outfit did not seem like it was regulation—especially the tight skirt that threatened to liberate her large thighs as she bent over seductively in front of Jerry and clucked something in Spanish.

No, it was business as usual.

"Where's Gregg?" Jerry called in my general direction.

"I'm not sure, late?" I suggested.

"Late! There's no excuse to be late!" he boomed. Jerry was nothing but a taskmaster.

Gregg, however, was a guy who once got me a whole hard drive full of Japanese hentai for my birthday. He was one of those guys who you saw in the hall and really wanted to like because he was different from everyone else in the office, but you also didn't want to talk to for too long because he was different from everyone else in the office.

Gregg was into some weird shit.

"I want someone on the phone with Gregg right now! We've got deadlines and he's not helping," Jerry commanded Aisha, his new secretary, who was having a pretty interesting first week. She was accompanied by what I was sure was a member of a Korean boy band. As she stood up, pulled out her cell phone, and dove into the hall, her companion followed, quickly trying to hold the door for her, which she in turn tried to force closed behind him.

"Now," Jerry said, clearing his throat, "I don't want anyone to make excuses for why things aren't getting done today," he batted away the playful fingers of his chica and continued, steely eyes forward. "This is still a place of business and it will always be that, no matter what!"

I shot my hand up.

"Yes, Goddamnit, this isn't elementary school!" he shouted.

"Sorry Jerry," I said, also clearing my throat, "But don't you think we should maybe — "

"No!" his voice echoed like a shotgun across the room.

All eyes were on me. I gulped.

"I'm just saying maybe today isn't - "

"I said no, Goddamnit!" Jerry stood and slammed his palm on the table, which caused his girlfriend to burst into a clap. "Today, we are a business, just like yesterday, and just like we will be tomorrow! Today is no different!"

I leaned back in my chair and nodded. My redheaded friend pulled a pack of bubblegum from her purse and popped a piece into her mouth. Jerry was right about one thing. Just like any other day, I wished I wasn't there.

***

Aisha wouldn't look me in the eye on my way out of the conference room.

"How's Gregg?" I asked.

"He's fine!" she said, bolting for the conference room.

"Is he coming in?" I called after her.

She turned, looked at me and darted her head down as her friend put his hands on her shoulders and began to massage them.

"No, he's spending the day with his mother," she said, and pushed the man's hands off her, slipping into the conference room where Jerry was trying desperately to fend off the advancing woman, now crawling over the table. I sighed. Gregg had the project decks for the latest campaign we were both working on, and I needed them to finish the package.

I sighed again because I knew Gregg's mother had died a few years ago.

***

I couldn't work; sitting in my office was bothersome. My redheaded visitor didn't come onto me as much as others seemed to, but still, having her in the room, smelling like soda pop and unabashedly planting her feet on my desk as she sat across from me, exposing her shorn lady parts, made me sad in a way.

"Is your real name Starr?" I asked her. She shook her head in a way that didn't really say yes or no.

"Where are you from, Starr?"

She tossed her head back and let out a sigh of frustration.

"Sorry," I said, trying hard to think of another topic of conversation. But I gave up when Starr hiked up her skirt and began to pleasure herself openly.

There was a knock at the door. It was Tim from sales. He held a cup of coffee and was alone.

"This yours?" he asked, nodding towards the now moaning Starr.

"I guess," I said with a frown.

"You, uh, you do it yet?" he asked.

"No!" I said, shocked. "Why would I do it with her?"

"Well, I mean," Tim shrugged his shoulders and nodded at the furiously masturbating porn star in my office.

He had a point. I had chosen her out of some sort of shallow desire for sexual gratification, so it did make sense. But now that she was here, in the flesh—the pale, bumpy, zit-marked flesh—it didn't seem right.

"You're a lucky bastard," Tim said. "I went out and got laid last night."

"I'm lucky?" I asked, confused.

"Yeah!" Tim said, "I bagged some fifty-year-old cougar with stretch marks and called it a night. Now you got her and I got nothing."

"I guess," I said, trying to find the benefit. "But how long is she going to be here?"

"She eat?"

"Not so far."

"Then she's invincible."

"What?"

"People are talking about how you can't kill them. They

throw them off buildings, shoot them, blow 'em up. Nothing."

"What the hell?"

"Crazy." Tim stepped a little further into the office to get a better view of Starr as she began to climax. "You mind?"

I shrugged and gestured with an open hand, telling him to be my guest.

"Jesus," Tim marveled. "You know they say that's just piss?"

"Goddamnit," I said with disdain as I realized I'd need to get a new chair from the overflow space on ten.

"You lucky fucker," Tim said, shaking his head and making for the door. "Hey, did you see Kyle?"

"No."

"Fucker came in with six Polish chicks."

"Six?"

"I know, I can't believe he came into work."

"Ah, that's because he's on the Ferguson job," I said.

"Oh shit, yeah, that's a doozy," Tim said, almost spilling his coffee as he leaned over to see Starr start up again.

"Alright, see you later." Tim nodded at me and smiled at Starr before he left.

***

I pulled my lunch from the fridge and found a place at the table. Tripp the IT guy was the only other person in the room. Well, that and our friends. His was a platinum blonde wearing some sort of armor and carrying an oversized sword. I'm not sure how they let her in the building with that, but then I remembered I'd heard that Carl, the security guard, and the rotund woman had left the building earlier.

"Hey Tripp," I said, sitting down.

He glared at me and took another bite of his sandwich.

"Who's your friend?" I asked.

"Fuck you," he said, tossing his sandwich down and making for the exit.

<hr>

I was instructed to finish the project with or without Gregg and so, in a vain attempt to make up the missing decks, I threw together a few samples of our design templates as best I could remember without Gregg's distracting influence.

"Too flashy," Jerry barked as I stood in his office. "We're not MTV!"

He tossed the specs down on his desk and I reached for them with one hand while the other fended off Starr's advances.

"I feel like our color scheme could use an update," I suggested in defense. "I was just following my instincts on this one and I don't think we should be so rigid all the time."

"Look, kid—" Jerry began, but was cut off by a loud thud coming from his closet. My eyes darted toward it, but his stayed locked on me, silently telling me to ignore whatever was behind that door trying to get out.

"I've been in this business a long time," he continued, "and in all those years I've never once thought about updating our color scheme. You want to know why?"

"Why?" I placated him.

"Because I know how to stay in my lane. And if you want to get somewhere in life, let me give you some advice. Keep your head down. And for the love of God, don't do anything because you *feel* like it's a good idea. Just do what you're told and collect your paycheck."

"Okay," I said after a moment. But I couldn't say anything more because Jerry jumped out of his chair when the closet door splintered under a Herculean thrust that was sure to take the door down on the next attempt.

The whole thing seemed to excite Starr, who was rubbing

her hands vigorously up and down my thighs. I was too consumed with anger at Jerry's dismissal to notice but the sudden threat of a charging BBW shook me out of it and I moved Starr behind me.

"Have Gregg look at these tomorrow. See what he can do with them," Jerry said, tossing the folder back at me as he went to move the cabinet behind his desk in front of the closet door.

"Sounds good," I said as cheerfully as I could manage, and let the impending fight Jerry had on his hands be my only satisfaction.

<hr>

As the day came to its inevitable end, it dawned on me how surprising it was that so many people showed up to work. Randy in accounting showed up with a man dressed as a plumber and he managed to get all his work done regardless. I saw at least ten Scarlett Johanssons. Frances in sales was with half the cast of that new reality show everyone was talking about, and the quiet girl in HR sat peacefully for most of the day on the front lawn with a young man who stroked her hair and hummed old rock 'n' roll songs. On the whole, I was strangely pleased to see everyone with their own unique type of visitor. Some of us were more extreme than others, but it made me wonder what we all had to be ashamed of.

As I walked across the lobby at the end of the day, I looked at the various incarnations of people's secret desires and I chuckled. Here everyone was, with exactly what they wanted, at least for a moment. These visitors were probably some of the purest and most confident expressions of our wants and needs that we had ever made in our lives, and we were ducking our heads to the ground.

I looked at Starr as she walked next to me, her high heels clapping along the lobby floor, and I put my arm around her waist. I brought her in close and I looked at her. Her hollow eyes, tired like mine. Her pulsating nostrils, breathing in the same air as me. She was a pure thought, a pure desire. And after a lifetime of being told that I shouldn't act on what I want, I decided I wasn't ashamed of her. I pulled her red-painted lips to mine and embraced her for all to see.

Her tongue forced its way into my mouth and it tasted like cigarettes. Her hand grabbed my crotch and yanked on it violently. I tried to pull away but she wouldn't let me. People began to stare as I danced with her in a struggle to get free. She tore my shirt off and ran her long sharp nails across my chest, pushing me towards a bench. I landed hard and she straddled me, her body easily exposing itself. I looked around and saw others with grins on their faces and watched as they grasped their partners and began to dance with them as I was. The lobby floor of my building quickly turned into an expression of bliss that would make the night clean-up crew's job a lot harder. We howled like animals and our cries of passion lifted us across the divide of our inhibitions.

I didn't sleep much that night. Starr had an insatiable desire that I did my best to satisfy. But at around four in the morning, I passed out from pure exhaustion on the living room floor. Just before everything went dark, I could feel Starr climbing on top of me for another round, but when I woke up the next morning, as the sun crawled across the floor to meet me, she was gone.

My phone was dead, long abandoned in the heat of the night, so I turned on the TV and watched a disheveled news anchor report that all the visitors had disappeared. This phenomenon was totally unexplained. It had happened in every city and every country, and the leaders of those countries had no answers. Instead, we all reveled in the outcomes.

Some of those same leaders were suddenly out of power, embroiled in scandals their visitors had triggered. A record number of divorces in a single day were filed, while at the same time a record number of new marriage licenses were applied for. The internet was full of theories ranging from plausible to crackpot, but the videos of visitors saying and doing any manner of things far outpaced the conspiracies in popularity. It wasn't every day you could make a video with your favorite influencer or K-pop idol in your living room trying to seduce you. Incidentally, Scarlett Johansson was suing twenty million people over the sale of an authentic sex tape and was somehow also getting a new reality show.

As I sat in my living room naked, the sun having met me on the floor, I decided I wasn't going into work today, and I wasn't going into work tomorrow. I was going to take a few days off and figure out what I was doing with my life. I didn't want to do a job that didn't fulfill me. I didn't want to compromise my passions for a paycheck. More importantly, I didn't want to go back into a building where I had so recently participated in a mass orgy in the lobby.

No, I was going to do something I really liked. I grabbed my laptop and opened up a new search.

Starr Rogan, real name.

DAY JOB

Eli needed a job—any job.

He had been unemployed for what seemed like a very long time, even though it had only been a few months. His life had hit a snag, and he was ready to take whatever job he could just to pay the rent on his crappy apartment. But now, he was literally stuck. He sat in a small room no bigger than a shipping container with nothing in it but a table and chair, and an old cathode ray tube TV on a cart like they used to wheel into the classroom when the teacher was sick. Its power cord snaked across the laminate tile floor to an outlet next to the only door in the room. Above that was a light that was currently off and a wall clock whose hands crawled across its face like the world's worst windshield wipers failing to wash the hours away. The only other thing of note in the room was the sign above the TV that read: "Please Keep Your Eyes on The Screen. Report Any Unusual Activity."

But all of that was far less confusing than what was actually on the screen: an unchanging image of trees. Maybe it was a forest somewhere but it could just as easily be a park or someone's backyard. The branches swayed in the wind.

From time to time a bird would cross the sliver of sky visible at the top of the screen—the most compelling thing that happened in an otherwise monotonous image.

He had been staring at this for hours in the tiny windowless room, dutifully following the simple instructions. When he'd first arrived, he walked into the nondescript warehouse on Cermak, wearing the gray button-down shirt and black tie he'd gotten from his uncle Sal as a graduation present, and apologized to the woman behind the thick glass window for being late. She didn't seem concerned, and only tapped the laminated sign taped to the orange formica countertop that read: "Please Leave All Personal Items with Reception."

Eli handed over the leather laptop bag he had slung over his shoulder and watched as the woman placed it in a cubby hole behind her. Then she returned to the window and tapped the sign again. It took him a moment but Eli realized that she wanted *all* his personal items. Reluctantly, he handed over his phone, wallet, and keys. He even gave her the crumpled receipt for the bagel and coffee he had bought at the Dunkin' by the Division Blue Line stop on his way down there.

Two months ago he had quit his office job in a fury of self-importance. He had been tasked with filing paperwork at a law firm in River North. He wasn't trying to become a lawyer by any means, but the temp agency assured him that this part-time job would lead to "something bigger." He definitely needed something bigger if he was going to make a dent in his student loans. It turned out that the bigger job was just filing paperwork full time and occasionally getting coffee for the partners. He'd managed to stay there for six months, and then when he realized he had just become a glorified errand boy, he quit to save what little self-esteem he had left. But after two months of living off the high of his bold decision, he found himself back in the same temp agency looking for a way to pay those monthly installments and get the creditors off his back.

"This one might be great for you," Melissa, the work-placement agent at Greatness For Hire with the short brown hair and the smile that always made Eli feel better about being in there, told him. He liked Melissa and could see himself being friends with her, or maybe even more than friends, but considering his precarious employment and financial situation, he thought making a move on the temp agent would only add to his problems.

He was told it was an analyst job, which excited him because, once upon a time, he had gotten a two-year degree in Systems Management from the junior college in his home-town after his high school English teacher told him he was good with computers. Maybe this was the time for that degree to finally be put to some use.

The truth was, Eli never really knew what he wanted to do. One day, while he was still living at home, not that long ago, his dad had said, "Why don't you just do *something*?" Strangely this had been some of the best advice Eli had ever gotten. Most people wanted him to make a grand decision or find a passion he could dedicate his life to, but he didn't have anything like that and was never the type to dedicate himself to anything. So lowering the bar to "something" had an odd, calming effect on him. After that, he didn't feel so shameful about his eclectic employment history.

A few months later, after driving for about every food delivery app there was, he saved up enough money to move downtown and got a small one-bedroom apartment in Humboldt Park for a price that all his friends told him was too much for the area. He was feeling pretty confident, and added a few more hours to his driving time to make up the difference. However, after almost a year, he found that the economics of gig work were a bit different when you were not only paying rent, but also bills and a loan on a Systems

Management degree you weren't using. That's when he started looking around for something less automotive-based. His friend Angelo, who he'd known in high school and now lived just a few blocks from him, suggested he look into temp work.

He'd shown up that first day dressed in his best clothes, the gray shirt and black tie, and filled out a pretty standard application. That's when he first met Melissa and she gave him the rundown of their process. Pretty soon she emailed him, he started at the law firm, then quit the law firm, and found himself standing in front of the counter with the glass window on Cermak. He felt strangely like he was being processed for a prison term. The woman wrote down all the items he had handed over and stuck the little slip of paper to the metal clip over his cubby hole. She reached under the desk and pulled out a sheet of paper. It was one of those white, yellow, and pink types of papers that allowed the text to be copied to all three. She slid it in front of Eli and handed him a pen that was attached to the counter by an overworked chain.

Eli scanned the page and knew what it was immediately. All those months of filing papers at the law firm taught him to recognize a pretty standard non-disclosure agreement when he saw one. He was agreeing to not speak about the nature of his work to anyone or face termination and possible legal action. The secret here was that no one ever actually took legal action against small-time employees. They just filed away the paperwork with their lawyers so they could cover their bases in case something did happen. Most of the time they just fired the employee, gave them a generous severance package, and went on with their life. It had become standard enough with big companies that it had kept him employed for six months and in the process nearly driven him crazy.

He scanned the document and was about to sign when he saw a clause at the end he had never seen before.

XIII. Employee understands that The Company retains the right to pursue all actions necessary to maintain the terms of this contract and Employee waives all rights to retribution.

Eli looked up at the woman and smiled. He tapped the clause with the pen. "This should be all *legal* action necessary, right?"

The woman didn't speak. She reached forward and tapped the signature line at the bottom.

"They're not going to, like, kill me if I accidentally say something?"

The woman only looked at him. Eli shrugged and signed the paper. He figured this was just a typo; he saw them all the time, and any lawyer worth their salary could get around that one. He slid the paper back to the woman. She filed it in a drawer and turned to a metal fixture on the wall with slots for small rectangular cards. Eli looked at the file she had put the paper in. He had assumed he would get a copy, but that apparently wasn't the case.

The woman pulled out a time punch card and she tapped the top where it asked for his name. He took the chained pen again and wrote his information down. The woman glanced at his handwriting before sticking the card in a machine that did the titular punching.

Eli followed the silent woman through a set of doors large enough for a truck to drive through and into a long hall with several other truck-size doors. At the end of the hall was a human-size gray door with no markings. An ancient-looking number pad was on the wall next to it, and the woman quickly entered an impossibly long series of numbers, each analog button giving a reluctant click.

Inside was the room with the TV and the image of the trees. Eli was directed to sit at the table and the woman pointed at the sign.

"You want me to sit here?" Eli asked, but the woman only pointed to the sign again. Without waiting for a reply, she closed the heavy metal door and Eli could hear the clicking of the number pad faintly on the other side.

He took a seat and looked at the slightly distorted image of the trees on the old tube TV with a curved glass screen. When they swayed in the wind, he could see the leaves breaking as they crossed the scanlines used to generate the image like an electronic tapestry.

After an hour, Eli could feel his bladder begging him to relieve it of the large Dunkin coffee. He glanced at the sign that asked him to keep an eye on the screen and decided it was worth it to find a place to satisfy his bladder. He went to the door and tried to pull it open, but it wouldn't move. He tugged on it hard, assuming it was just stuck but from the way the frame shook, he could tell it was locked. He knocked lightly on the door but got no response. He wasn't about to piss in a corner so he took a seat again and held it.

Another two hours passed and he started to feel like this was a joke. Nothing had happened on the screen except a flock of birds had flown by. Was this "unusual activity?" He guessed it depended on what was normal activity in this circumstance. Getting locked in a room with a TV showing a single image of the woods was certainly unusual activity as far as he was concerned. Perhaps whoever had concocted this prank would think the normal flight pattern of migratory birds was unusual. He briefly wondered if Melissa knew about this and was punishing him for quitting the law firm. Was this what they did to unruly clients? Was he paying for his lack of drive and motivation?

After another hour of contemplating how he had found himself in this torture chamber, the lightbulb above the door turned on with a buzz. Eli looked at it for a long moment, waiting for something to happen, but nothing did. He glanced at the TV again and found it unchanged. By this point, his bladder was full enough that he had been determining which corner would be most suitable, but in a moment of insight he stood and grabbed the door handle again. The door swung open freely.

He approached the counter where the woman sat reading a tattered paperback with the painted image of two lovers in the throes of passion on the cover. She looked up at him with no sense of remorse or even recollection about locking him in that room for hours. She found his timecard and put it into the machine where it punched another hole and then she retrieved his belongings from his cubby hole. Without a word she went back to her novel.

Eli had planned a whole series of curses and condemnations for this woman but her casual indifference to his plight took all the oxygen out of his anger. He eyed a faded sign for the men's room and decided his time was better spent there. As he was relieving himself, he resolved to never come back to this place. He'd call Melissa in the morning and have her relay his anger and make sure she never sent anyone else there as well.

***

The next morning Eli woke up to find $1000 in his bank account from BirminghamDale Inc. He hadn't been told what the rate for the work was when he agreed to do it but $1000 was so ridiculous that it must be a mistake. He called Melissa and after clearing his throat so it didn't sound like he'd just woken up, asked her if this was a rate for the day or for the month. She told him that as far as she knew it was a daily rate, but that the company had been very tight-lipped about their payment structure because, as they said, "The nature of our work is very sensitive."

Eli had no idea how to take this, but $1000 was hard to argue with. He had gone to bed last night fully intending never to return to that warehouse on Cermak, but now he found himself putting on his shirt and tie and looking at the train schedule. He got a bagel at the Dunkin' but skipped the coffee to save his bladder.

When he walked into the lobby, he found the same woman sitting there, now a few inches further into her book. She looked up when he approached and reached for his timecard.

"Can I ask you a question?" Eli asked, but the woman ignored him. He decided to ask anyway. "Is the payment I received a day rate or is it for the month?"

The woman turned and tapped the sign on the countertop. Eli handed over his laptop bag, wondering why he had even brought it, and set his phone, wallet, and keys on the orange formica.

"I just want to make sure it's not a mistake or something."

The woman continued to ignore him as she put his things in the cubby hole and attached the itemized list to the metal clip.

"I mean, I'm not mad, obviously," Eli laughed. "I just need to plan my budget, you know?"

The woman punched his card and exited the booth for him to follow her.

"Is there a supervisor I can talk to? Or someone in charge?" Eli asked as he followed her down the hall.

The woman punched in the long code on the number pad and opened the door. Eli followed her in.

"Maybe there is someone I can call to sort it out?" Eli asked as the woman looked at him and pointed at the "Keep

Your Eyes on the Screen and Report any Unusual Activity" sign. She shut the door and Eli heard the number pad clicking again, shutting him inside.

Just to be sure, he jiggled the door handle to check if it was locked. He sat at the table feeling dejected and looked at the curved image of the trees. He was taking a gamble here, but it was only four hours—he hoped—and then he'd find out if he was getting paid again.

As the time went by, he found himself mesmerized by the unchanging image on the screen. It was a simple thing really. Sitting here for four hours looking at a TV. He had spent more time looking at a TV than this in the two months between jobs. Of course, those images were more riveting, but maybe this could be therapeutic, if he let it be. The idea of getting $1000 a day *was* therapeutic to him for sure. At that rate, he could have all of his loans paid off by the end of the year. Soothed by this thought, he glanced at the clock and watched the minutes crawl by.

Exactly four hours later, the light above the door buzzed alive. Eli gave the TV one more glance to see if anything at all had changed—it hadn't. He opened the door and made his way back to the little glass booth the woman sat in and collected his things.

"See you tomorrow?" Eli asked, hoping to get some sort of response from her, but as usual he got none.

He checked his phone first thing in the morning. His bank account showed another deposit from BirminghamDale for $1000. He practically floated out of bed. How had he lucked into this? What the hell was he even doing to deserve this?

He quickly got dressed and left the house, making sure to leave the laptop bag at home, and bolted for the train. The sooner he could get there, the sooner he'd be done for the day and the sooner he'd be $1000 richer and with half the day still left. This, he thought, was truly the definition of doing *something*.

Inside the little room, Eli put his feet up on the table and leaned the back of the chair against the wall. He started humming a song to himself that he hadn't heard in years, and before long he was singing it out loud. It occurred to him that this was what crazy people did when they were locked in a cell.

<hr>

"You do what?" his friend Angelo asked over drinks. Eli explained the job to him again, and Angelo thought he was joking. It hadn't taken as much convincing as he'd hoped, but after Angelo pestered him enough, Eli decided to tell him, despite (or in spite of) the questionable NDA. After assuring him it wasn't a joke, Angelo didn't seem as excited for him as Eli would have assumed.

"That's some messed up shit," was all he could say and told Eli to be careful. Eli thought he had found some hack in the system, but as he was defending the job, he realized how strange it must sound.

"Any job that locks you in a room for four hours isn't a real job," Angelo explained. "And if they're paying you that good it's because they don't want you to think about whatever fucked up stuff they're doing."

Eli laughed it off and offered to buy the drinks. But Angelo wouldn't let him and soon he found himself alone at the bar wondering if Angelo was right to be wary of his new employer.

Before he left for work the next day, he called Melissa and asked if he could meet up with her later. She agreed and suggested they meet downtown for a coffee on her lunch break. When he met her at the small restaurant that had been downtown since the '30s and had terrible coffee but was quiet, he asked her what she knew about the company that was hiring him.

"I've never heard of them," she said, tearing open her second pink packet of artificial sweetener and pouring it in her coffee. "It's only ever been emails."

He told her about the locked room, the TV, and the woman who never talked.

"That actually isn't that weird. Most of these big corporate clients hire a bunch of temps for meaningless work—no offense." She smiled at him and took a sip of her coffee. "And to be honest, they rarely last long, so I'd be happy to have it while you do."

The meetup didn't last very long either. Melissa said she had to get back to work but that she would look into BirminghamDale a little bit more and would let him know what she found.

"Sure, yeah, thanks," Eli said, taking a big gulp of his coffee as Melissa flagged down the waitress and asked for a to-go cup. "And if you do find anything, maybe we can meet up someplace with better drinks?" He smiled at her and she smiled back.

"Well, even if I don't find anything, that still sounds fun," she said and poured her coffee into the to-go cup. "See you then!"

Eli decided to sit in the small shop to finish his coffee. He pulled out his phone and did a simple web search on the BirminghamDale and found an innocuous website with pictures of smiling people and windmills. He dug a little deeper and found some articles that were just as frustratingly vague. They were an international conglomerate based in some small town in downstate Illinois that seemed to have their hands in everything. More than likely, they were so large that appendages grown out of mergers and acquisitions had gone unnoticed for years. It was anyone's guess what they actually did, and a complete mystery what Eli's job entailed. Although, he thought, perhaps it was only a matter of time before someone noticed and cut the offending arm off. He decided to take Melissa's advice and be happy to have the job at all before anyone noticed.

When he showed up to the warehouse the next day, the woman behind the counter had moved onto a new book. This one was a different flavor from the last. Still in the romance genre, but the cover featured a tall hairy creature holding a supple young woman in his arms. Eli craned his neck to read the title and caught "Bigfoot" and "Lover" between her fingers.

"Looks interesting," he said as he placed his phone, keys, and wallet on the countertop. The woman made no response other than to set the book down so she could grab his timecard.

"Hey, do you work for BirminghamDale or are you also a temp?"

She punched his card and moved for the door.

"I'm only asking because I'm curious about what we're doing here. I didn't know if you knew anything."

He followed her down the long echoey hall, trying to think of some way to get this woman to speak.

"So if I do see something, who do I tell?"

She punched in the numbers on the keypad.

"Come on," Eli insisted. He refused to walk into the room. "That's part of the job right? It's on the sign." He pointed to the sign.

The woman only stared at him. They played a game of chicken until Eli finally relented and walked into the room. The woman pointed up at the sign.

"Yeah, yeah, I got it." Eli sat behind the table.

The screen, just like the woman behind the counter, hadn't changed. In fact, so much of this job was monotonous that it took him almost three hours to notice the scratch marks on the floor. When he did, he walked around the table and knelt down on the tile floor to inspect them. They were faint, but he was pretty sure they hadn't been there before. It looked like something had been dragged across the linoleum from the table to the TV. But there was nothing in the room that was heavy enough to make those marks. It occurred to him then that he was not the only one who used this room. He was only there four hours a day, and that left twenty other hours for it to be used for anything else. He mostly came in the morning, but he had been given no set schedule and two days ago, after getting drinks with Angelo the night before, he had come in the early afternoon, nursing a hangover, and the same woman was behind the counter, reading her book. Now he was wondering if she ever left.

When the light above the door came on, he moved down the hall quickly and found the woman almost done with the Bigfoot book.

"Hey uh, I don't know if it counts as unusual activity but there were some scratch marks all over the floor in there."

For a brief moment, the woman looked up at him. It was the first time that anything he said seemed to register with her. But it passed by, and she handed him his things and punched his card.

The next day, Eli could smell the fresh scent of cleaning solution in the room and saw that the tile had been replaced in the areas where the marks had been and the whole room had been buffed clean. Any hint of the aberration was gone.

"How long you going to keep this up?" Angelo asked. Eli told him he didn't know how he could quit. The morning after the floor had been replaced, he woke up to $2000 in his bank account. The next day it was back down to $1000, but the message had been clear.

"I gotta go meet this guy," Angelo told him. He was having a security system installed in his apartment after he'd caught someone trying to jimmy open the living room window a few nights before. It'd been a rough week for Angelo, and Eli felt bad complaining about his job to him. The restaurant he'd been working at for years let him go without a reason and the tires on his car had been slashed. Eli offered to help him pay for it, but Angelo seemed offended by the suggestion. He told him he could talk to Melissa about getting him a job at the place he was at but Angelo wanted nothing to do with it. That was the last time he'd talked to Angelo. When he got out of work a few days later, he had about two dozen messages from friends asking him if he'd seen Angelo. He'd missed his sister's birthday party and when his parents got into his apartment, they found the bedroom window smashed and Angelo missing.

Eli helped put posters up around town and kept up with posting about his missing friend online, but so far no one had heard from him. A thought entered his head, and he tried to ignore it. But sitting for hours in that room, staring at the endlessly unchanging trees, a lot of thoughts crept into his mind that he'd rather not have. As far as he knew, Angelo was the only one he'd spoken to about this job in detail. Sure, other people knew he had a job, but he hadn't told anyone else exactly what the job was.

That wasn't exactly true, he realized. One other person knew about the job.

He called Melissa over a dozen times before he finally got a call back from an unknown number. He was relieved to hear her voice even if she was whispering. Melissa asked him to meet her at the restaurant again and even though she refused to say the name out of some paranoid fear, he knew what she meant.

Downtown late on a Sunday night was a different place. The nine-to-fivers were safely back in the suburbs and the tourists were sleeping on flights back to wherever the hell they came from. The "L" rumbled above him proving that some life was still in the city as he walked down Wabash Avenue. The restaurant wasn't empty, but it might as well have been. He found Melissa sitting at a booth facing the door, a cup of coffee gone cold in front of her that she was pouring sweetener into anyway. She saw Eli the moment he entered but didn't beckon him over. When he sat down he asked her what was wrong and she told him she'd been looking into the company that hired him.

"It took some digging but I was able to go into our database and see that they used to hire with us under another name." She whispered across the table. "Huntington International Security Services."

"Security?"

"Yes. Your job used to be listed as a security job but now it's just called an 'analyst.' But that's not the strangest part." She reached down to the seat of the booth and with a few glances around the room, she pulled out a folder with some printed papers in it. "Huntington was hiring through us for years before they were acquired, or consumed, by Birming-hamDale. We don't keep exact records on every interaction that happens, but when a company hires an employee full time, we get a termination of services letter, which under normal circumstances, just means they're taking over employment and our records stop. But I did a little more digging and found, well, this."

She slid the folder over to Eli and he opened it up. Inside were several printouts from various government websites of missing people. Their faces smiling at him from last-known photos that many of them didn't know would be their last.

There were also several employment records from Greatness For Hire where Melissa had circled and highlighted the same names on their rosters.

"What is this?" Eli asked, he could feel his hands already shaking.

"Those are all the people we sent to work for that company. All of them are missing or presumed dead." She pulled the cold cup of coffee across the table and began tearing up more pink packets of sweetener to feed to it.

Eli looked up at her and smiled. "Is this a joke?"

Melissa grabbed his hand. "I don't know how much longer you have. Ever since I started looking into this, I've been followed, my emails are being read. I think they know."

Eli pulled his hand away. Melissa looked insane with her eyes bugging out. She was surrounded by spent sweetener packs and it was clear she hadn't showered in days.

"Please Eli, listen to me. You are in extreme danger. You have to get out of there."

Eli said he would be careful and he urged Melissa to take some time away from work. It was clear she was not well. She gave him the folder and told him to study it, look into it, prove her wrong. He said he believed her even if it was just to get out of there.

He took Monday off and on Tuesday he tried calling Melissa again. When he couldn't reach her, he called Greatness For Hire and they told him she had moved back home. No contact info. He hoped that was true. She looked like she needed it. But what if she hadn't? What if her paranoia was warranted? He shook the thought away before it infected him too. Angelo's disappearance had rattled him. Anyone in his position would be looking for answers. But why should he jeopardize himself, his income, his security, over rumors? He had just two more months before his debts were paid off. All he had to do was stick with it a little longer. He looked at the file folder on his desk. Inside was a tale of misery for everyone involved. But he wouldn't let that happen to him. He checked his phone and saw a payment for Monday even though he hadn't shown up. This had to be a mistake, but at this point he wasn't sure he cared. Just a few more months, and then he would be free.

But still, maybe he didn't have all the answers.

When he arrived at the warehouse, he wasn't sure what his plan was. He had left all of his belongings in the car so that there could be no mistake. The only thing he held was the folder clutched between his fingers like a sacred tome. The woman sat at the counter. She had finished the Bigfoot book and was now reading something with an alien on it. His long spindly green fingers were wrapped around the midsection of a barely-dressed blonde woman. But Eli wasn't there for that. He stood in front of her for a long moment and waited for her to tap the sign. When she did, he laid down the folder nervously. But when she reached to grab it, he held tightly onto it. Her eyes looked up from the yellowed pages of the book with contempt.

"Can I ask you something?"

She tapped the sign and he nodded.

"Yeah, I know. But I'm just wondering if you remember any of these people?" He opened the folder and showed her a spread of names. She kept her eyes on him, and then slowly her pupils drifted down to the paper. Eli waited for a reaction. He studied her face, waiting for any sign of recognition, or even realization, that he had figured out some dark secret. But she had none.

"I'm not trying to accuse anyone of anything. I just wondered if maybe you could let someone above you know that there are some suspicions going around that I'm not sure they're aware of. And that maybe, if they knew, they could clear it up."

The woman looked back up at him and then she snatched the folder and slid it into the cubby hole. She pulled out his punch card and finished their typical interaction.

"Okay," Eli said feeling a slight burn from the force of the folder being ripped out from under his fingertips. "Let me know if anyone has any questions."

The woman set down the book and exited her booth so she could lead him down the hall. Eli followed her and didn't say anything when she pointed at the sign and locked him in the room. He looked for more scratches but the floor still looked brand new. On the screen was the same damn image. As the hours went by, Eli felt like he might actually be going insane. What in the hell was he doing here and what the hell was he looking at?

Right when he had that thought, he saw something move on the screen. It wasn't the trunk of a tree swaying in the wind or the leaves billowing in the breeze. It was something peeking out from behind one of the trees, looking at him with two large dark eyes.

Eli stared back at the thing, trying to discern what it could be. He watched as it extended two long skinny limbs out from behind the trunk and moved slowly towards him. His eyes struggled to place the spindly creature into any taxonomy he was familiar with, but he didn't have time to decide on anything as suddenly it was moving much more quickly towards him. Eli jumped back, but felt the strong grip of cold hands reaching out of the curved screen. They pulled him in, and he found that he was screaming. He clawed at the floor, his fingernails dragging across the tile leaving bloody marks as he was pulled effortlessly towards the TV.

The woman behind the counter put her book down and took the timecard out of its slot on the wall. She punched the last time on it and wrote "terminated" below it. She opened a drawer and placed it with the stack of others inside. She picked up her book but hardly had time to read another paragraph before the front door opened and a young woman dressed like she was here for a job interview entered. She smiled as she approached the counter, and whatever she said didn't matter. The woman tapped the sign and waited for her to comply.

THE CRAWL SPACE

Jane had been meaning to clean the house for a long time now. And not just a quick tidy-up, but a true deep clean. The kind of clean that would pry loose years of accumulated clutter from the nooks and crannies of the house she and her husband, Alan, had lived in for twenty-four years. Now that her boys had grown up and moved out of the house, she wasn't going to let anything get in her way.

They had gotten the house at a price that would be amazing by today's standards with some of the money Alan's mother had given them as a wedding gift. Alan liked to remind her how hard his mother had worked to save up that money, and even though Jane was a co-signer on the mortgage, she often felt like she was a squatter in the big old Victorian on the corner of Hamilton and Grace in Jackson, Illinois.

At the beginning, Jane had many plans in her head that would bend the home to the shape of her grand designs. She wanted people walking by to stop and admire the house, wondering about the lives of the people who lived there. However, as the years went by and the debris of life fell in her path, the home became merely a functional instrument meant to serve a purpose to her and her family. Now, something had changed. She missed her children, but when she found herself in the quiet peace of the kitchen in the morning, sipping a cup of tea and looking out across the deck and to the small garden beyond, she hardly remembered she had spent the last two decades of her life chasing after their wants and needs and cleaning up the messes left in their wakes. They were now, thankfully, many hours away, making their own messes.

Looking through a box of forgotten photos in the upstairs hallway closet, she felt the weight of the memories. Photos were stacked on top of one another haphazardly—school recitals, church camps, holidays, family picnics, and a ski trip they had taken when the kids were still too young to ski. Alan was beaming at the camera in a winter jacket he had spent way too much money on. She wasn't in the photo.

Several more boxes of photos were stuffed in this one closet and soon she was done hauling two decades of life down the stairs and into the basement.

She considered just putting the boxes of photos in the room her oldest son had turned into a practice space for his band, which now amounted to only a few discarded guitar cables and some amateur graffiti sprayed onto the walls. But they'd had some flooding issues in the past, and that didn't feel like a safe place for the memories. This was a problem Alan swore he had taken care of when his good friend Trench lined the walls with plastic sheeting and discarded gutters. Trench's contraption did help stop most things from getting soaked, but the basement was still damp enough to give Jane a slight sinus headache whenever she spent too much time down there. And in the fall, when the rains came, Trench's contraption was less effective. Even now, she noticed a pool of water had formed in the corner of the band room. She reminded herself to have Alan call Trench about that.

This left her very few options for where to put the boxes.

There was Alan's "man cave," which was really just an old couch, a TV, a stereo, and some posters Jane had pleaded with him not to display in the rest of the house. But Alan would give her a hard time about a pile of random boxes in his space. That left the laundry room, the unspoken-for domain of Jane, where everyone dumped their discarded belongings. A space she had not asked for, nor really had any say over. There was a small square door halfway up the wall next to the washing machine. Jane had always assumed it was access for plumbing or something else she never concerned herself with. The door had a metal handle, and the only thing holding it shut seemed to be the friction of its age and the misalignment of its hinges. When she gave the handle a firm tug, the door popped open like the cork of a pressurized bottle. A warm, humid breeze hit her in the face. There was nothing to see, save for the dirt floor and ancient-looking brick walls that were crumbling into sand on either side. She leaned her head in and peered deep into the space where it receded into the underbelly of the house and saw only darkness. It was dry, though, and seemed like a good refuge from the basement's moldy dampness.

She placed the box of photos inside along with a large tub of old trophies, meaningless certificates, and a box of random computer cables. The door seemed to eagerly close itself like the mouth of an animal and it provoked a primal fear that caused her to pull her hand away instinctually. She looked at the door for a long moment, expecting more to happen. But nothing did. In fact, she felt better now that the burden of the clutter had been lifted.

That night, she told Alan the basement was leaking again and he told her it was "impossible." He was fussing over the hamburger meat he was pulverizing into a mush of wet beef and grocery store-brand spices. Later he would describe this process of creation to his buddies like he was passing on some ancient wisdom before that night's football game.

"It's just condensation from the temperature change," he attempted to explain.

"The temperature in the crawl space seems fine," Jane added.

"The where?"

"The crawl space. In the laundry room."

"I wouldn't go messing around in there."

"Why not? Where does it go?"

Alan looked over at Jane and shrugged.

"Under the house," he said with an annoyed scowl.

Jane asked for more clarification but Alan was more interested in getting the grill started than discussing it further and left her alone in the kitchen.

Jane continued on her warpath of cleaning and by the end of the week, all the closets had been cleared and organized. She had found coats at the back of the vestibule closet that had been around since the time she and Alan had been dating. How they had managed to stay hidden back here all these years, she didn't know.

Arms full of coats, she grasped the metal handle and pulled the crawl space's door open. The release of pressure pushed the door toward her just as it had before. The air inside was still warm despite the chilly weather. Jane paused, squinting into the darkness. She stood there, puzzled, for a few long minutes.

The crawl space was empty.

Hadn't she put something in here? Those things? Those… well, she actually couldn't really remember what she had put in there. There was so much stuff that it was all blurring together. If it was something she really wanted to remember, she told herself, she wouldn't have put it in here anyway.

She piled everything into the dark hole in the wall, including the vacuum Alan had gotten them when they moved away from his hometown after the wedding. He was convinced that the "big city" would be dirtier than his small town, and that they'd need a vacuum with a good filter to make sure everything was spotless. The only problem was, he'd stayed up drinking and bought it off a late-night infomercial. The damn thing didn't have any suction and two of the wheels broke off a week later. She hadn't wanted to tell him it was a waste of money because he was very proud of himself, and now his great triumph had been at the back of the vestibule closet since the 2000s.

Jane had finally convinced Alan to have Trench come by to look at the basement. She stood in the old band room, looking at the badly spray-painted logo of her son's band, and waited for Trench to inspect the drainage system he had "come'd up with m'self"—a fact she had no trouble believing. He diagnosed the problem as the walls being too porous and his makeshift system not being able to handle the influx of water brought on by the storms that were very common in the region. She already knew this, but Alan had always insisted they let Trench handle the basement because "He'll do it for a quarter of what the big guys will." Jane always pointed out that he'd only do a quarter of the work as well, but Alan never took her seriously. Trench advised they let him seal the whole thing with another one of his concoctions.

The next day, Trench was there with a bucket of awful-smelling black goo that she had no doubt he'd "come'd up with" himself. The stench permeated the whole house, so she decided to move her reorganization efforts outdoors for the day.

Many armchair historians in the neighborhood had informed her, while walking their dogs, that the detached garage had once been a carriage house. "That's probably why it's taller than a normal garage," they would explain in a half-informed, half-I'm-just-making-this-up tone. Usually Jane would nod and point out that the house was built in 1908, technically a bit shy of the true Victorian age, but being in the Midwest, thousands of miles from anywhere Queen Victoria had ever lived, she was willing to count it.

Thankfully there were no Victorian period experts walking their Dachshunds today and she was able to open the wooden sliding doors on the garage, *née* carriage house, to let in the crisp afternoon air without distraction. Alan had thought he would turn this into a workshop, but instead, it had ended up just being a repository for whatever project he had gotten excited about before dropping it like a TV show he lost interest in mid-season, leaving her to finish alone.

It would be nice to have space to park the car in the garage when the snow came so she began clearing space. The one useful thing she'd discovered was a giant garbage can that now became the proud owner of the many boxes, broken pieces of furniture, and instruction manuals that littered the workbench and the ground. Anything that felt too expensive to donate or throw away, she put back in the original boxes and hauled them inside to the basement.

Trench had made good progress slathering the black goo along the walls. He didn't even hear her descend the stairs with the boxes of tools over the noise blasting from his paint-splattered stereo. When she opened the door to the crawl space, she found it empty again. A foul stench wafted over her this time, and she felt dizzy for a second. The sealant Trench was using must be bleeding through those porous walls just like his music, she thought as she set the stack of boxes on the lip of the dark space.

She stared momentarily into the void and felt strangely like she had forgotten something. There was nothing there but the smell and the crumbling brick, but she still felt at a loss. Like a word was on the tip of her tongue, she had a feeling she couldn't quite describe—an echo of that fear she had felt the first time she had looked into this abyss. She hesitated to close the door but she told herself she was being silly, it was just some old tools that no one would miss.

She slid the boxes across the dirt floor and watched them for a moment. Nothing happened of course. Only the warm air washed over her like waves crashing on a shore or like some lung pulsing with life.

Then she shook her head. That was some strong stuff Trench was using, she thought and closed the small square door.

A few days later, Alan was in the basement acting out the hell he'd give Trench when he got ahold of him. He'd been away for the last few nights on a work trip, and when he got home he found that the whole house smelled like Trench's goo. Alan took one look at it and pulled his shirt over his nose. "Why did you let him do that?" he yelled at Jane.

"Trench is *your* friend. I didn't hire him."

He stormed away to open every window he could.

He eventually left the house altogether, saying he was going to The Cork for dinner because he couldn't stand to be in the house with that awful smell. He didn't invite her, but that was okay with Jane. He always said the food at The Cork wasn't "as bad as everyone says." She would disagree on that part but it wasn't the food that kept her away. The Cork was one of the only bars on the strip next to the small art college's campus. Its wood walls and ample bar seating made it feel more like a frat house than a place to get dinner. Jane always suspected Alan enjoyed the youthful feeling it gave him more than the food, but she never found a good way to say that. Really, she just enjoyed the time alone.

A few days later, Alan dragged Trench down to the basement. His anger had subsided since his first discovery, but by that point, he had made such a show of being upset, and since he'd taken his lunch hour to come all the way home to deal with this situation, he was damn well going to yell. From what she could hear, Trench assured him it was going to work as soon as he was finished and that the smell would go away in a couple of days. Alan wanted an example made though, so he told Trench to leave and that he'd fix it himself.

Jane was pruning her mums on the deck when Trench climbed into his old Toyota truck, looking dejected with his radio in hand.

"Where's my belt sander?" Alan asked from behind her. "I'm going to need it to get this crap off the window frames."

"I don't think you have a belt sander," she said. "Did you check the garage?"

She watched the red drain out of his face as he remembered that he had never owned a belt sander as far as he could recall.

"There's no room in the garage." He stumbled through his confusion. "Your car—it, uh, takes up all the space," he said.

He mumbled something else about hiring a "real professional" to take care of the basement because he didn't have the time anyway. "I'm going to have to work late tonight," he said like a limp balloon releasing its last bit of air. She watched him walk to his car, where he stopped to give the garage one long look before getting in.

A week later, Trench was at the front door again, apologizing profusely about his last visit.

"It's really not as big of a deal as Alan made it out to be," Jane assured him.

There had been strong storms all week and the whole county saw up to ten inches of rain, which caused the basement to flood even worse than before because Trench had not been able to finish what he started. After a few more angry calls, Alan had determined that a professional would be too expensive and too time-consuming, so he agreed to let Trench come back and finish. "For a pretty good price," Jane was assured.

Trench inspected the walls in the former band room and in Alan's man cave. He slathered more of the black goo in the spots he appeared to have missed. He explained again that this wouldn't have happened if he'd been allowed to "get her done."

"What's in there?" Trench asked, pointing his flashlight towards the square door halfway up the laundry room wall.

Jane explained it was just the crawl space and that they didn't use it for much. Trench rubbed his jaw and decided that he better check it out "just in case."

"Oh, no, I'm sure it's fine," Jane found herself protesting. "We never use it. It's just a bunch of dirt."

Trench laughed, showing his missing teeth. "I don't mind getting a little dirty," he said. "And Al wanted me to make sure I did her right."

She smiled as she reexamined his stained clothes and stepped out of the way.

He popped the door open and took a few steps back at the rotten smell that hit him in the face. He let out a whistle and said he might as well check for "anything dead" while he was in there. And fulfilling his promise, he shimmied up into the hole and crawled inside.

Jane could hear him whistling at the smell the further he got in. "Ah boy, whatever it is, it's way back in here," he said, his voice growing fainter.

Then she heard him screaming.

Jane gripped the edge of the opening and yelled inside to see if he needed help, but she got no reply. She couldn't bring herself to crawl into the foul-smelling hole after him.

After a while of staring into the darkness, her grip on the edge loosened. She couldn't remember why she had come down there. There was nothing in the crawl space. She had a feeling like she was meant to be doing something there, but couldn't recall anything at the moment. She closed the wooden door and went back upstairs.

"What do you mean, you don't know whose truck that is?" Alan demanded when he got home.

Jane looked out the window at the little beat-up Toyota truck with all the tools in the back. She had no idea how it had gotten there. She didn't remember seeing it arrive or who might have been driving it.

Alan didn't believe her but he made a big show of complaining about the neighborhood and how it was being taken over by "hoodlums." He called a tow service and when it arrived, continued the performance by going outside to "make sure it gets done," which Jane imagined was very enjoyable for the man winching the Toyota onto the flatbed.

Later, when they sat in front of the TV, she noticed a distant look on Alan's face, like he was worried about something.

"What's wrong?" she asked.

"Are we supposed to be doing something today?" he asked, his eyes fixed on the screen.

"I don't know what you're talking about," Jane said.

Alan excused himself to the back deck to make a phone call and Jane heard him talking quickly to someone in hushed tones. It was ridiculous that he thought she couldn't hear him, but she guessed he also thought she couldn't smell the cigarette smoke as well. She had told him before that she didn't care if he smoked every once in a while. They had both smoked "every once in a while" when they were younger. In fact, they met while having a cigarette outside the bowling alley in Alan's hometown where she had been attending a friend's birthday party. Their first conversation was about how they normally didn't smoke but they like to have one "every once in a while." But as the years went on, those "once in a whiles" became fewer and fewer, and now she thought Alan kept it to himself because he assumed she would judge him or something worse. She had never given the impression she would, but it had become something that the two of them just stopped talking about. Something that had been their little secret was now just his.

A week later, Alan was leaving for work when Jane asked, "Did you ever figure out what we were going to do about the basement?"

His face pulled together in an expression like she had spoken in a foreign language.

"What?" he asked incredulously.

"The basement? We were talking about getting it fixed? Because of the flooding?"

Alan was in a hurry and distracted by the day ahead. "I don't know if we've been talking about it. That basement has been leaking for years. If you want to have someone come look at the basement, be my guest. Just make sure you get a good price." He gave her a perfunctory kiss on the cheek as he headed for the car.

She supposed he was right. The basement walls had leaked as long as they lived there. She was sure they *had* been talking about doing something but it was now just one of those tasks that she would have to add to her list of things to do to bring this house back to how she imagined it.

Alan hadn't come home last night. Usually when he was working late she would get a call. Sometimes a text. But last night she had gotten nothing. When she woke the next morning and he wasn't home, she called him, but got no answer. She called his office but they told her he had left early the day before. She was half considering calling the police when he finally came in the front door. Concerned, she confronted him and he told her he had been at work late. When she told him she knew that wasn't true, he said he wasn't working at the office but off-site. By this point she already knew he was lying. It was just a matter of how soon he would admit to it.

He made another one of his big shows of telling her she was overreacting. The reason he hadn't called was because he lost his phone. "I can't call you if I don't have a phone!" He stormed into the bathroom to take a shower. He was late for work and the last thing he needed was to be questioned by her. "You don't know what I do for you!" he yelled from the bathroom. "You don't know how hard I work! I don't need you to give me the third degree about everything!" he yelled, and slammed the door.

Jane felt a little foolish for her concern about him but still, something nagged at her. Alan went to work, skipping the normal goodbyes, and Jane sat with herself thinking about all of this. She did some more cleaning and found it a nice distraction. But this task only kept her mind occupied for a short time before she went back to the puzzle that weighed on her. Why had Alan disappeared for almost twelve hours and seemed upset that she would be concerned about him?

From the bedroom window she saw a red four-door Kia pull up to the curb. A young woman, in her thirties, Jane thought, jumped out of the car and walked up to the mailbox. She opened it and slipped something inside. She looked around nervously and then got back into her car. Jane watched her drive away, and then made her way down the stairs and outside to the mailbox where she found Alan's phone.

A few days later, when Alan came home from another long night at work, something that seemed to be happening more and more, Jane showed him the phone. He was relieved for a brief moment to see it, but then she told him how she had gotten it and what she had found. He quickly admitted to the affair with the waitress from The Cork, as if this would be the end of it, but she knew the password to his phone, a simple four-digit code that unlocked a story of a years-long relationship that came to a head the night Alan went missing.

"I didn't have a choice," he said, as if this would absolve him of the consequences. "For Christ's sake, I can't have another kid. Not now. Was I supposed to let her keep it?"

Jane said she wasn't looking to critique the problem he had created. It was his mess, and like the house she had been working on diligently for months now, he had cleaned it up the best he knew how.

"It was supposed to be easy," Alan explained. "We would

go to the clinic, get it taken care of, and then it would be done. But it took longer than I expected, and she didn't want anyone else to know. If I hadn't forgotten my damn phone…" He looked at the piece of metal and glass like it had caused all the chaos. And in a way, he wasn't wrong. She had looked inside it and, like a dark talisman, seen what damage it had wrought. It was a sordid tale of flirtation and desire that Jane would probably have enjoyed reading about in some novel or watching on one of the TV shows Alan never liked to finish. But now it was happening to her, and the text messages and voicemails were not as alluring and dreamy as the shows or books.

It was his idea to get divorced. She could see that he thought he would make a life with this young waitress and live out the fantasy foretold in the messages on his phone, one he had seemingly failed to achieve in their relationship. Had they always felt this distant from one another or was this new? Hadn't they wanted to build a life together? Hadn't they wanted to experience the things twenty-five years of marriage had brought them? She couldn't remember exactly what those things were but she knew they were there. She wondered how many cigarettes he'd shared with his waitress and promised her he only did it "once in a while." And then one day he packed up a small moving truck's worth of stuff and went off to live at an apartment he had rented on the north side of town. Then Jane found herself alone in her late Victorian home in a town the Queen had never heard of.

Her crusade of cleaning had resulted in very little visible change to the house. You really had to dive into the hidden places to see the differences. Her friends, who she couldn't recall ever being so concerned for her, began stopping by with more frequency. When she told them how she was feeling, she said just enough to make them feel like they were helping. What she didn't tell them was something in her had changed. Somewhere in those deep hidden places, something was different.

Her sons had reached out, but she didn't know what to tell them and they didn't know what to tell her. They were living their own lives and neither seemed interested in getting involved in this drama that suddenly appeared in their past. They spoke to her like strangers reading a headline about some far-away event.

After a few weeks of shuffling around the house like a ghost, she decided it was time to really do something. Everywhere she looked, she was reminded of Alan. He had been a constant presence in her life for almost thirty years, and now it was like a light switch had gone off and he was no longer there. Except he *was* there. Some of his clothes were still in the closet. His shaving cream and toothpaste were still leaving stains in the medicine cabinet. When she opened the kitchen cupboard to grab a mug for her tea, she was confronted by commemorative glasses inside from the various conferences he'd been to throughout the years. And many, many photos dotted the walls of the house chronicling their life together. So she packed these things up in great handfuls and carried them down to the basement. Armful by armful, she fed them to the gaping maw halfway up the basement wall. And with every deposit, she felt lighter. She felt better. The deep space in her heart that she had given over to Alan was being cleaned out.

He came by the house one day in November when they got their first snowfall of the year. He was wearing a sweater and a corduroy blazer. His ears were red from the cold, but the first thing she noticed was that he hadn't shaved. It wasn't the disheveled scruff of a man here to beg for forgiveness, it was the weeks-long growth of a middle-aged man who thought the beard made him look less square and somehow more youthful despite the prominent flecks of gray and the white hairs spilling down from behind his ears.

He wasn't interested in having a conversation. He explained that he had simply come by for his winter jacket and she hadn't been answering her phone. She didn't remember getting any calls from him, but she wasn't interested in conversation anyway. She almost didn't want to let him in. He felt like a stranger to her in a way now. What did she really know about this man? Had it only been a few weeks? She felt like she hadn't seen him in a lifetime.

He seemed unsure what to do, standing outside the home he technically still owned half of. She finally let him in and he facetiously asked permission to go to the closet, which she dismissively allowed. He dug around in there for a good long while until he returned to the kitchen where she was making a fresh cup of tea. The kettle was almost boiling when he stepped into the room and asked, "Have you seen my winter jacket I bought for that trip with the kids?"

She thought about it. "I don't remember a jacket. Which trip with the kids?"

"We went on a trip… somewhere, and that's where I got the jacket." As he grasped for the words, his tone turned urgent.

She had no idea what he was talking about.

He grew flustered as he seemed to forget why he had come over there at all. "If it's not here then I don't know why I even came over. I don't want—I just need the jacket."

She turned the burner off under the kettle. "I've been cleaning. Maybe I put it in the crawl space."

"The crawl space?" he asked. "Why would you put it in the crawl space?"

"It's dry in there." That was the only reason she could think of.

"Dry? It's dirty and full of God knows what." His face turned sour. "That jacket was expensive!"

She couldn't imagine why he was so upset about a jacket from some forgettable trip years ago, but he did a lot of things she didn't understand.

"Are you sure you put it there?" he demanded. She could see the flush of anger flooding up over the top of his beard.

"I don't know. I've been doing a lot of cleaning up. I can't keep track of where I put everything."

"God damn it," was all he could say and he pushed past her to the basement door. She could hear his angry footsteps pounding down the wooden stairs and his deep exhales as he let out the frustration at having to do this chore at all. She imagined he had thought this would be a quick trip, and now here he was, hunting around in the basement for something he probably should have just forgotten about.

She poured the hot water into the mug and let the tea bag float on the top for a moment. Then she lifted it up and submerged it again into the water, watching the blooming dark red stain spread out over the surface. From the kitchen she could see out of the front door where a red four-door Kia sat running. In the passenger seat was the young waitress, her face glowing from the light of her phone screen in the overcast, snowy day. For a brief moment, she looked up and saw Jane standing there. She looked lost and confused, as if she had just woken up from a dream.

And then Jane heard screaming.

She walked down the stairs with her steaming cup of tea and saw the door to the crawl space hanging open. The smell coming from the door was rancid, and the dry hot air flowed out in the sharp cold that had permeated the rest of the basement. She looked into the deep hole for a long while and listened to the cries and struggling sounds coming from within.

After a moment, she couldn't remember why she had come down there at all and shut the door.

Three weeks later, Jane was lighting candles around the house to give it that thick pine tree smell. The large Christmas tree in the front room was doing most of the work, but she wanted to make sure the rest of the house felt festive. She had always admired the many homes in the historic neighborhood she lived in that would go all-out during the holidays to bring the joy of the season to anyone who walked by. There were many architecturally unique and beautiful homes on this side of town, and Jane had always felt her 1908 Victorian was one of them.

She'd put so much work into the house these last few months that it felt good to sit in her home and watch the passersby admire her decorations. It was her home. Always had been. And now that it was finally clean, there was room inside. Room for new possibilities. Room for new memories. Room for her.

THE TALK

THE BOY WAS GETTING OLD ENOUGH THAT, SOONER or later, I would have to have "the talk" with him. He wasn't my son, but I was all he had. His mother had stumbled onto my farm years ago, alone and desperate. Normally, I don't trust strangers, especially after things got so bad that we had to put a fence around the property. But a pregnant woman in these bleak times was hard to turn away. Plus, I must admit, I was feeling quite lonely too, and in those days, I hadn't accepted yet how bad things had really gotten.

She was in bad shape, whoever she was. I did my best to care for her with the few supplies I had, and we made it through the birth, but just barely.

She cried when he was born, not the kind of tears I'd assume a mother typically sheds, but true, sorrowful tears. She didn't need to tell me why. Considering all the trouble boys had brought to the world, well, I cried too.

After that, she didn't stick around long. She said she didn't trust two men to care for her. Some might view it as a cruel act, but I understood. I tried explaining that I had managed to live out here on my own for many years without issues, but she'd just shake her head, saying it was only a matter of time. As much as I wanted to argue, I knew she had a point.

My mother had brought me here when I was a young man to protect me from the world, the same reason the boy's mother had brought him. Things were quieter now, but in the old days, we lived in constant fear of someone coming to take what little we had. Even worse, we feared one of us might be lured away from the meager life we had managed to cling to.

Mother had died years before the boy and his mother arrived. If she had been alive, his mother wouldn't have made it past the first gate. And now, here I was, raising another eager young man despite my misgivings, the same way my mother had raised me all those years ago.

The boy had grown up on the farm, never leaving it, the same as I had. He learned to garden, tend to the animals, and manage all the intricacies that came with a self-sustaining life on open land. I saw him get bigger and stronger, and at the same time, saw how old I had become, and realized how little time I had left. I tried to teach him as much about the outside world as possible, but there came a point when my teaching felt like cruel teasing. He yearned to leave the farm and experience all the wonders of the world that he had read about in the books I kept around the house, but I forbade it. Things had changed an awful lot since those books were printed. However, he was growing older and stronger, and I knew that soon, I wouldn't be able to stop him from doing what he wished. I had to let him know why he could never leave this place.

I found the boy in the barn, working on the old tractor. He believed he could get the motor running, and I wouldn't be surprised if he could. He had a mind for machines and that scared me. After all, machines had gotten us into this mess.

I asked him how it was going, and he told me about the

parts he wished he had and wondered if we could go find them. Maybe, he suggested, we could even find some other people who might have them. I reminded him, for the hundredth time, that there was nobody else around. When he asked how I knew, I simply replied that I just did. Even if I wanted to know for sure, I would never go looking. He didn't press me on the issue, having heard this response a hundred times before. But I could see the spark in his eyes and the thought that passed behind them. I knew he was thinking about looking on his own one day.

I asked him if he wanted to know why we never left the farm. He didn't say yes, but I knew he had wanted to know since he knew enough words to start asking. Finding a chair in the corner, I looked out across the field at the sun, which hung low in the sky. I asked him what he already knew, and he responded that he knew something bad had happened to the world. I told him he was correct about that, but the worst part was that it started off as something we thought was so good.

This was, of course, the hard part. There was so much to tell a boy so quickly becoming a man, with so many thoughts running through his mind. However cruel I felt I was being, it was nothing compared to the torture his own body was subjecting him to at this age. He was ravaged by a desire for something he knew very little about.

He had, of course, found the magazines I kept around the house. He knew what a woman was and what that meant. So when I went on to explain the birds and the bees and everything in between, he told me he already knew all about it. But despite his defiance, he still had questions, and I answered them the best I could. If there was something I wasn't sure about, I told him I didn't know, but I'd find a book somewhere in the house that we could find the answer in. But as I'd suspected, this did little to satisfy his curiosity. So I pressed on.

I told him it was okay to be curious, but he had to be careful. It was our nature to be curious. Curiosity had helped us invent so many amazing things like the tractor, or the windmill that powered the lights in the house, or the water pump that gave us groundwater. We were eternally curious creatures, but in the end, when we thought we had found the ultimate answer, all we had found was the answer to our destruction.

He wasn't following me, so I explained as plainly as I could, or as I understood. I told him that some men out west had created something that deeply satisfied them—more than anything ever had before. Machines had industrialized the world to a point of almost complete bliss for those lucky enough to reap the benefits. But all that was gone now, replaced by our final creation. Man had created the ultimate device to satisfy his most basic needs—the needs of the body, the needs of the flesh. In any way or form you wished it, this machine could provide. And as it evolved, it would offer forms of satisfaction beyond what one could ever have even dreamed. Once a young man myself, I explained, I felt the pull of this creation. I, too, had been tempted by its allure. But I had seen the destruction it wrought and what damage that temptation could bring about.

The boy didn't speak. I think he understood what I was saying. His face tried its best to hide his wonder. He knew I meant this as a cautionary tale, but his body was on fire with fresh chemicals at the thought. I'm sure he was thinking of those magazines around the house. I wish I had done a better job of hiding them, but in the end, there was no point. He would figure it out on his own one way or another. The drive of curious desire is like no other.

I told him this was why he couldn't leave the farm. The machines were still out there. Once the genie had been let out of the bottle, it couldn't be contained. Just the same, once man had found a shortcut to his desires, nothing else mattered. And so, the world crumbled. Industries failed, governments toppled, and the slow churning of life ground to a halt. Sure, some people tried to step up and take control. But the system we had established wasn't ready for nearly half of its participants to suddenly quit. And the machines that had undone the world continued their work, unaware of the damage they had done, their desires being only to fulfill their programming—an ouroboros of completion that was to eat us alive until there was nothing left.

The boy didn't have any more questions. His face was flushed with embarrassment as I left the barn. The sun was now dipping below the horizon, leaving a splash of orange and purple across the sky. Out here, you could see for miles. That was one of the reasons my mother chose this place. Even in the dim light of the setting sun, it was easy to see the woman approaching the first gate. She looked as young as the boy's mother had all those years ago, except this one wasn't pregnant. They never were. This one smiled at me with eyes full of possibilities. The shape of her body and the way her dress barely clung to her shoulders spoke more than words could to an old lonely farmer. I returned her smile and waved as I approached. The gate was electrified, but they had long since learned not to touch it. I grabbed the shotgun I kept in the gatehouse, and, without giving her time to speak, I took her head clean off and left only a spray of sparks and a spattering of mechanical parts on the main road. It was the quickest way to kill them. I was sure to clean up the mess so as not to attract more, or give the boy any ideas of where he might find parts for the tractor. But despite the fence and my aim, they would send more. They always did. And soon, it wouldn't be for me.

STILL HUMAN

I swore this ghostwriting job would be the last. It was for a socialite on the Upper East Side who had a series of romance novels about a woman and her horse. Apparently, it was a different woman in every story, but you'd be hard-pressed to tell. After skimming through a few of them to get the context, I started to draw a grand story of a woman who fell for a perpetual set of trainers and then dealt with their tragic deaths after a brief but steamy love affair, only to learn that the true love of her life was the horse all along.

Given the landscape of trashy fiction these days, I was hoping she was looking to finally write the human-plus-horse romance she seemed to always be hinting at. But instead, she handed me an outline for a new series she was writing about one of her more popular male love interests, who escaped the death loop of her other stories and now lived in Australia on a cattle ranch. I told her I knew nothing about Australian cattle ranches, but she assured me she had left all the relevant details in the outline. And as a good ghostwriter who was simply looking for a paycheck, I looked up the rest online, watched a few documentaries on Australia, and covered the inaccuracies with plenty of sex.

That was the job, more or less: take the scrawled lines of a rich older patron and turn them into more prestige for them to haul around at galas or dinner parties or whatever they do with all that time they're not spending writing. I should be happy that the days of AI ghostwriters were behind us. After an initial boom—publishers thought they'd struck a gold mine, books without writers!—it quickly became apparent that AI still couldn't match even the most mediocre human. They said it would get better, and it did, but there was always something missing, no matter how expertly crafted the prose was. And not for nothing; a lot of people didn't care. But when the market became flooded with AI slop, the human-written trash floated to the top.

I made my living as the trash that didn't sink. At the very most, it was a fine excuse for me to put off my own writing, which was a nice way to think about how I hadn't published anything of my own in almost a decade. Not for lack of trying. I'd gotten lucky with a novel I wrote right out of college, a time-and-place story about a boy, right out of college, who was writing his first novel.

This very original idea, nevertheless, struck a nerve with Raph Guliardo, the patriarch of the Guliardo Publishing House and now the proud owner of a stone mausoleum in Greenwood Cemetery. Raph had apparently seen something in me that his sons didn't. David and Julian saw GPH as a clearinghouse of talent ripe for distribution to the various low-bar markets looking for cheap content. GPH had never been prestigious in its own right, but Raph had an eye for talent and had been the first to sign many authors who would later go on to great acclaim—very often elsewhere.

Their biggest fish, and the one that led all the pitch meetings, was Bradley Hughes, the author of *Verisimilitude in Repose*. The late 2020s had been a heady time, and Hughes seemed to capture it eloquently and, more importantly, succinctly. Raph had been the first to see that and the first to tell Hughes that he should take the offer from Random House for his next book.

Hughes followed up *Verisimilitude in Repose* five years later with *Carhart Diaries*, and then *The Mind, The Body, The Mouth, and The Company*, which won him his second Pulitzer, the National Book Award, and every other honor they could bestow on him. Somewhere in there, Raph found me, and I was just as excited by the possibility of being discovered by the man who had discovered Bradley Hughes.

But there was never a Pulitzer for me. Instead, I was trying to figure out if it was realistic for a man to sleep with a rancher's wife in a horse stall at the height of an Australian summer. The answer, it turns out, doesn't matter.

I wonder if Bradley Hughes ever felt this way. He went almost two decades between *Carhart Diaries* and *The Mind, The Body, The Mouth, and The Company*, the former of which had a terrible movie adaptation that Hughes refused to endorse. *The Mind, The Body, The Mouth, and The Company* eventually got its own movie, but it was much more well-received and even got nominated for a Best Picture Oscar. It lost to another adaptation, *Brickstone Manor*, which was based on the Broadway show of the same name.

I never saw either. I did see *Carhart Diaries* and didn't think it was as bad as everyone said. The book was damn near four hundred pages, so there were bound to be some cuts, but I thought they handled it well. Most of the backlash was from the setting change. The book took place in rural Nebraska but they set the movie in Texas because, I guess, the director didn't feel like Nebraska had the sufficient amount of Americana he was looking for, which of course undercut the entire point of the story. But I thought the acting was pretty good, and it was shot beautifully.

That was probably the last time I thought about Bradley

Hughes. After *The Mind, The Body, The Mouth, and The Company* lost the Oscar, he sort of faded out of public consciousness. Ironic in a way, as that story dealt with the aging process of a man in a world full of technology designed to keep him young. Hughes himself wasn't a young man by that point. Nearing his seventies and by now certainly well into his eighties—if he was alive at all—he seemed to be saying, through what would apparently be his final work, that death was something to be avoided and not celebrated.

The main character of *The Mind, The Body, The Mouth, and The Company* accepts a life-saving treatment that keeps him alive far longer than intended. He watches as all his friends die around him and resigns himself to a life sequestered from a world that didn't want to be reminded of their own eventual deaths. He dies alone, which had been his worst nightmare. I guess I can see why it didn't win over *Brickstone Manor*, a musical about a group of college kids living in a three-flat apartment in Chicago in the early 2000s.

I don't know what happened to Hughes after that. I don't remember hearing about him dying, and I think I would have. The voice of a generation would at least get a passing mention, enough for me to stop scrolling past it on my news feed. I think I'd heard he'd gone into retirement somewhere on Long Island, and no one had heard from him. As far as I could tell, Bradley Hughes had disappeared.

That was, until Julian called me about a new ghostwriting job. The last name I expected to hear was Bradley Hughes, especially in the context of needing a ghostwriter. Perhaps he was ailing enough that he just needed someone to dictate? But why not just get a secretary or read it into a computer? I suppose he was old school. His generation was known for their aversion to new technology, considering how it had done them all so dirty. Either way, there was no chance I was turning the assignment down. If Bradley Hughes wanted me to write his grocery list, I'd do it, at least, out of curiosity.

The following week, I took the train to Montauk and was met at the station by a car that ferried me through the quiet streets, still suffering summer tourists. The trees were still green, with only the occasional brown and red of the approaching fall. The car, a driverless black sedan, lulled me into a hypnotic state with its calming music that seemed to be coming from every surface and which I hadn't bothered to turn off because it only enhanced the surreal feeling I'd had ever since leaving my apartment in Brooklyn early that morning.

I had assumed this was just an interview, but when they had insisted on an in-person meeting rather than a call, it seemed like Hughes had already made up his mind. I never got a satisfactory answer to "why me?" other than: Hughes had always trusted Raph and wanted to go through him rather than his actual publisher. I suppose he granted David and Julian the same trust.

The soft hiss of the door releasing and rising into the air, like a mama bird letting a baby out from under her wing, pulled me out of my trance. I looked up to see the sprawling cedar-shake-clad home with its salt-dusted shingles and several nautical flags flapping lazily in the easy wind. The fraying on the edges betrayed any sense of modernity.

The door opened, and a tall man in a white coat stepped out to greet me. He could have been a doctor—or just a housekeeper. No doubt Hughes had round-the-clock care, and I wondered if the situation I was walking into was going to be more dire than I had expected.

Was I here to bear witness to the passing of one of literature's greats? Was this a torch passing that I was certainly not worthy of? Had he gotten the wrong guy? There were half a dozen Brooklyn-based authors much more suited to the honor than this hired gun.

Despite my misgivings, I said hello to the man, who had that smooth, supple face of someone who had gone through the surgeries that seemed to be standard procedure these days when anyone turned sixty. They could do amazing things now. Gone were the days of stretched faces and propped-up wrinkles that made you look like a grocery bag with a broken jar of jelly in it. Now they could make you look ten, fifteen, even twenty years younger with hardly a sign. But even still, you knew one when you saw one. It was the uncanny defiance of time that existed only in the face while the rest of the body struggled to keep up.

The man showed me into a room with a sunken floor and a smoldering fireplace that had clearly been burning all morning with no replenishment. He asked me, through full lips, if I wanted anything to drink. I asked for water but stood in that room for almost twenty minutes and never got any.

Books lined the walls, and I was unsurprised to see some authors I enjoyed and even some I knew. What I was surprised to see was a first edition copy of my book. Well, the only edition. It never sold more than its initial print run, if that. However, the thrill of finding it in the sitting room of Bradley Hughes almost made it worth all the anguish it had caused in my life.

After a long enough wait, long enough that I almost wandered off to explore the rest of the house, a young man entered in a neat blue sweater and khakis, looking like the perfect college boy from a 1980s teen comedy. But what really struck me was how much he looked like Bradley Hughes on the back flap of the first edition of *Verisimilitude in Repose.*

I wasn't aware that Hughes had any children, but then again, I wasn't aware of much about his personal life—a fact I hadn't really considered until this moment. I knew of the man and his work, but that was about it. However, even for the son of Bradley Hughes, this man was young. He couldn't have been more than twenty, which meant Hughes was siring a new generation in his sixties. Not unheard of, but still not the norm, despite the advancements in medicine these days. More likely, I was looking at a third generation Hughes.

But to make things more confusing, or rather, disconcerting, the young man introduced himself as Bradley. I took this to mean Bradley Jr. or the third. But he offered neither clarification.

He was a warm boy who seemed to know more about me than I did about him. He had that off-putting way that some young people have that makes you think—no, makes you certain—that they are more intelligent, thoughtful, and sensitive than you are. That in all your additional years, you hadn't managed to acquire a knack for the world like they had.

Despite this, or maybe because of this, I was glad to meet this Bradley, and we talked for a good long while about writing. He was an author himself, and we talked a little bit about my work. It turned out it was his copy of my book in the small library, and to my astonishment, he was a fan.

I enjoyed my conversation with this younger Bradley so much that I'd completely forgotten I was there to meet his father, or grandfather. I remembered when the doorman with the off-putting face came back and whispered something into Bradley's ear. The young man said it was lovely to meet me, and I was shown the door. I did have the fortitude to turn and ask, just before the door shut in my face, "Is Mr. Hughes in good health?"

Bradley the younger put on a brave smile and said he had good days and bad days. I was happy to hear that today was a good day, despite not meeting him.

I climbed into the waiting car and let it lull me back to sleep as it wound through the twisting streets and broke out onto the main road, headed back to the city. If I was being honest, I wasn't sure who I had talked to today. It couldn't have been Bradley Hughes himself, and yet I left with the feeling that it had been.

It was a full two months before I heard from Bradley

again, younger or older, and by that time, I'd almost finished another manuscript for my main benefactor. That last one I wrote in two weeks, and it had already hit the top of the charts, and she was hungry for a sequel. I had a bit more free rein on this one, as it was a rush job, so her typical multi-page outline was now just an email with a few rushed thoughts.

I kinda enjoyed this one, if I'm being honest. The ranch came under attack by some thugs from one of the big neighboring corporate ranches, and our hero was forced to defend everything he had worked for in the first book. All of it was complicated by the fact that an old flame was leading the opposition and offering him power and money beyond his dreams.

I mean, it was still trash, don't get me wrong. In the end, our rancher stuck to his roots and fell for the girl who worked at the local bar, but I got to write a few action scenes, which are always fun. They won't let me write much more than descriptions of bodies and the clothes they're wearing— or not wearing, so a few thrown fists and some explosions were a welcome change.

I was actually in the middle of the climactic third act when Julian called to tell me that Bradley wanted to see me again. I told Julian that I hadn't actually met him and that I'd only spoken to his offspring. This seemed to confuse poor Julian, and I'm sure it was just a miscommunication given that there was another Bradley Hughes in the picture. Either way, I agreed to take the long trip out there again.

When I got to the house, I was told that Mr. Hughes was down by the beach. It was an unusually warm fall day, the kind that seemed to arrive just before a storm, and he had taken advantage of it to get some air. I was happy he was out and about because it meant it was likely a good day and thus an ideal time to meet.

When I got to the back of the house, I crossed the deck

and stepped into the sand, where I could see the figure in a dark coat standing out, looking at the horizon that was already darkening at this hour. When my footsteps became audible over the wind, he turned, and I was not unpleasantly surprised to see the young Bradley again. I said as much but added that I was expecting his father. He gave me a funny look, then he smiled.

He suggested we go inside so he could explain. I wasn't sure what he meant exactly, and I asked: "Is this about your father?" He gave me a look like I was a naive student who had assumed the wrong answer. I held in any excuses for my ignorance out of fear of them just confirming it.

We sat on the sun porch and watched the clouds roll in over the Atlantic. There would be rain soon. The man in the white coat with the odd face appeared with some drinks and a tray with two syringes on it. I didn't believe I was asked to come up here to do intravenous drugs, but it turned out they weren't for me. One after the other, he injected them into Bradley's arms. When they were done, he dutifully rolled down his sleeve and then held up his drink to me for a toast.

He toasted our partnership, and after taking my sip, I confessed my confusion to him finally. I told him that I was under the impression I was there to work on some sort of project with the elder Hughes. This got a small chuckle from him, apparently at my expense, because he apologized right away and told me he hadn't been forthright with Julian because he wanted to meet me first before he explained the situation. A situation that was delicate, complicated, and most importantly, private.

At that cue, I was served a paper from the man who had previously just been serving IVs. I saw that it was a pretty standard and buttoned-up NDA. I'd signed plenty of them in my work. A trapeze artist never gave the net any credit, and this was me, the net, agreeing to that.

I told him it was no problem and readily signed it, but

before he would accept it, Bradley insisted that I look it over. I scanned it and saw the normal things one would expect: I forfeit my right to authorship, I understand my name and likeness will not be associated with the work, etc., etc. But at the end of the papers, I saw a few new clauses that had something to do with science and human aging.

I don't think I possessed then—or now—the ability to fully process what I was reading, but the gist seemed to be that anything I saw, heard, or even said was not to leave this house.

Once the binding contract was accepted, Bradley excused his manservant and told me he'd have to start from the beginning.

In his own words:

I assume this has already occurred to you. If not, let me be clear. I am not the son or grandson of Bradley Hughes. However, there is a reason I look like he would have at this age and why I am here. It's a simple answer on the face of it, but obviously, it is complicated by any other metric. I am not the son, or grandson, of Bradley Hughes. I am Bradley Hughes. At least, in a sense, which is why the complicated answer requires some explanation.

It began after I completed work on The Mind, The Body, The Mouth, and The Company. *After it was published, I was approached by several groups that took an interest in the ideas expressed in the novel. It wasn't exactly all fiction, as most people could tell. Even then, we were seeing experiments showing promise around life extension, cell regeneration, and all kinds of things that would have been sci-fi just ten or twenty years before.*

What I was trying to say in The Mind, The Body, The Mouth, and The Company *was that these things were real, and we'd have to deal with them not only as a society but as individuals —that is, philosophically. What does it mean to live without death?*

What does it mean if the order of evolution is turned on its head? The book is a cautionary tale, but it is meant to provoke conversation, to outline a course that might allow us to see the roadblocks ahead.

The truth, of course, was that I had been thinking about this for years. I've never been afraid of death; I've just felt it was a nuisance that we could deal with. The body is just cells, blood vessels, and tissue —why can't we maintain that? The consciousness has never been shown to be anything but a confluence of the senses, so why could it not be kept intact?

As a result of this curiosity—and this book—I became aware of the edges of this world. New options became available to me that had previously not been known. I began work with several companies on technology to bring a person back to a prime age and keep them there indefinitely. It was not an easy task, and my being here is the result of many years of work.

The first problem was the repair. As I aged—as all of us age—our cells are ever dividing and copying themselves. With each successive copy, the cell and the information it contains degrade. Over time, we become harder to "read," like a set of instructions run through a copy machine hundreds of times. For a long time, geneticists have focused on repairing these cells. By adding information back in, they hope to reverse the process of aging by rejuvenating those cells, like dried sponges under fresh water.

But like those sponges, they are never the same. No matter how much water, there are always frayed edges, stains, and missing pieces that can never be recovered. The only real answer is to get a new sponge. That is where our work ended and the result you are looking at today.

Almost exactly ten years ago, this body was created from a cluster of cells and a sample of my original DNA. The growth was accelerated over that period to reach this age, where it is maintained and continuously rejuvenated.

As for my mind, that is another matter. While I would be conscious without my thoughts, my memories, my ideas, I would not be Bradley Hughes. I would be a very healthy copy of him, but that would be it.

Despite our extensive research, we have come to the conclusion that there is no realistic way to transfer the mind of a man into another body—not by biological means alone, at least.

At the same time that I became interested in the science of life extension, I also became interested in the science of large data sets and how language models can simulate human interfaces.

We've had chatbots and AI computing for decades now, but I wasn't interested in synthesizing all of man's knowledge into a friendly robot that could answer any question. I wanted to create one man: myself.

Over the last few decades, through a variety of inputs, I began working on a replica of my mind that could be loaded, via a powerful microprocessor, into my existing consciousness.

The conclusion of that project was what prompted the creation of this body and the eventual transfer from my mind to this body.

I was very glad I signed that NDA because I had a lot of questions. The basics of the situation made sense, insofar as they could make sense, but the thing I couldn't figure out was this: if Bradley Hughes had duplicated his body and copied his mind into it, why did he need a ghostwriter?

I got the answer after a few knowing nods from Bradley, who seemed to be anticipating this question. He told me the honest truth: there was still one problem they hadn't cracked in this top-notch procedure. Despite the years of work put into crafting the perfect replica of his mind, the one thing they couldn't create from scratch was the ability to do that one thing humans seem to be best at.

He couldn't come up with any new ideas.

He had all the passion, the knowledge, and the skill he always had, but the artificial mind he had created could only reference what it already knew, what it had already created. The ability to create something new, to take the creative leap it takes all great artists to see just past the edge of perception and snatch that thing out from the ether, was gone.

The irony, of course, was that this skill alone wasn't special or unique. The artistic world was littered with failed "new" ideas. It was the combination of the new and the skill to craft it into something presentable that gave you a Bradley Hughes. He was, like so many before him, a maestro of playing the unknown and bringing it into our world. Or at least he used to be.

He offered me a substantial payout for my help, which was to give him ideas for stories that he could then write—with my help, of course—and pass off as new Bradley Hughes work.

Why did he want to do this?

Turns out he was eying a bigger prize. The technology behind all this—the body duplication and the mind photo-copying—was going to do a fair amount of business, and what better mascot could there be than one of America's greatest still-living authors putting out new work? Imagine, they could claim, if we still had Twain, Hawthorne, or even Vonnegut. In fact, if the ethics weren't so dicey, I'm sure they'd try to bring them all back.

The arrangement was simple: we would develop and write the new work together, but upon completion, I would be strictly left out of the discussion. I had no issue with this as the money flowing into my bank account turned out to be good—more than good—it was fucking fantastic.

But when Hughes asked me if there was anything I wanted outside of the money, so help me God, I told him there was. I don't know why I cared, maybe it was the sense of possibility surrounding me, but I said, someday—not today and maybe not for a while—I wanted my own deal. A real deal with a real publisher.

My career was about as real as the body with a computer chip in its head in front of me so if I was going to prop up this figment of Bradley Hughes, then I figured we could both pretend.

Hughes agreed to my terms, and we shook on it. The manservant came back into the room, and a few more papers were signed. Hughes offered me a room for the night as the storm had finally landed, and the sunroom was being assaulted by millions of tiny pellets of H2O fresh in from the Carolinas. I told him that I'd prefer to sleep this revelation off in my own bed, and I could sense a bit of trepidation as I got into the car.

If he could, I think he would have kept me there against my will to ensure his secret. But I think there needed to be a little faith here, considering what I was being asked to do. And besides, he knew he had me. I gave him the damn carrot before he even thought about it. If this went well, we'd both be realizing something we thought was impossible.

I told Julian that I was done taking any other work. He asked me for more details on the Hughes job, and I told him I was under NDA. This caused a bit of a stink at GPH, and I was put on a conference call with Julian and David to "discuss" the situation. I think the stink was the smell of their fifteen-percent.

One of their writers was working with Bradley Hughes, and they were expected to sit back and not make anything off it? When they invoked the clause of their contract, I walked away. Hughes sent an army of lawyers to deal with the contract, which turned out to have lapsed years ago. No one had noticed, as we all figured there wasn't any hope for me beyond horse fiction.

Regardless, they got a tidy sum of cash to keep them

quiet, and when I ran into David at a party a few months later, he was very happy to see me. That was one of the last parties I went to in Manhattan for a very long time. One of the last I went to in the city at all, as a matter of fact.

I'd resisted going out to Montauk very often, even though Hughes kept an open invitation. I wanted to keep a fair amount of distance, but even I found the days spent out at the house intoxicating as I found myself the personal idea factory for Bradley Hughes. And so, three months into our partnership, I agreed to move into the guest cottage permanently.

Hughes had a car for me that I could hop in and tell it to take me anywhere. But we really hit a groove with the work once I moved out there, and I didn't feel the need to return to the city at all.

I pitched him half a dozen ideas, and he asked me questions like a creative writing instructor. He poked and prodded them for themes, ideas, and characters. It was stimulating. It was like I was building a bridge, and he was there to keep driving heavier and heavier vehicles over it. Each time it would collapse, I would build a stronger one. It was, of course, always up to me to make that leap to the next iteration.

I could see him trying as he got excited, and I could see him fail, which was almost worse. The ideas he came up with always lacked something. They weren't bad, exactly, but they weren't great.

I hate to admit it, but I found this enjoyable. To be in a room where I was besting Bradley Hughes. I don't think this drove a wedge between us, but I could see it bothered him. So much so that he learned to pull his punches because he knew they would never land.

By the beginning of the following year, we'd outlined concepts for three new novels. We'd worked out such a rapport that we decided I would take the initial pass at writing the first of the three, *A Youthful Revelation*, a cheeky nod to the project as a whole that was a spiritual sequel to *The Mind, The Body, The Mouth, and The Company*. Once I was done, Hughes would come in and make it more his style. This was all new territory and none of us knew the best way to work. But I know we both enjoyed the process, and the companionship.

I got the strong impression that the man in the white coat with the odd face—whom I found out was named Brutus—wasn't much of a companion. He was supplied by the Norwegian company funding all the procedures and experiments that had become Hughes' daily life. It turned out Brutus was a doctor, mostly, but also a kind of guard. He never said as much, but it was clear that Hughes wasn't allowed out of the house under any circumstances—not at least until the book and the return of the prodigal son was revealed later that year.

At some point during our liaisons, through some massive influx of cash, Hughes had bought both properties to the east and west of him. This afforded him more space to roam and, as a side benefit, gave me an entire house to move into.

When I wasn't writing, we would take long walks through the grounds and along the beach, always with Brutus trailing us, to discuss the projects, or just anything at all. It was still strange speaking to a relative boy as if he were my elder. Which, of course, he was, and he comported himself as such, but the juxtaposition was hard to get used to.

I felt myself wanting to comfort him with the wisdom of age regarding his troubles, but I was always confronted with the reminder that I was the less experienced one when he gave me a simple, knowing smile, or offered up some advice that only age could bring. Whenever we finished a long walk, I would often complain about my knees and the price of my own age, almost as a way to get back at him for his stolen youth.

Nevertheless, he would let me have it by calling me an "old man" or something even less original. My usual retort would be to tell him I was "still human," with a mischievous smile that dared him to call his lumbering manservant over to throw me out.

But he would laugh, and later, after a long brainstorming session, when he stood to stretch his back and twist his neck, resulting in several pops and groans, he would look at me with the same devil-may-care smile and simply say, "See, still human."

It was on one of our walks that I finally asked the question that had occurred to me when this opportunity first presented itself, but I had deliberately pushed to the back of my mind with the strong sense of opportunity. Questioning my own worthiness was never difficult for me, but as our walks down the freezing beach became more frequent, and frankly more friendly, I found myself afraid to ask if there was some reason he chose me other than his respect for old Raph. What if he realized he had never asked himself that and changed his mind?

But when it came spilling out of me on one of our last walks down the beach before it turned too frigid to risk it, Hughes attempted a lie, but part of his condition, I guess you could call it, made him an awful liar. He told me he thought I had a unique voice that hadn't been given a chance. Which, of course, wasn't true. I had been given a chance, and my "unique" voice got lost in a sea of other "unique" voices.

I told him he was a bad liar and then I told him why I thought he had chosen me. I knew I had some talent—I could turn a phrase here and there—but my true skill was as a pastiche. I was a chameleon who could slip into any slot and give you a passable version of something else. Truthfully, I wasn't that different from Hughes in his current form. We were both empty vessels looking for a conduit. In other words, we were convenient tools for each other.

He tried to dissuade me from this, and I reminded him again that he couldn't lie. But I assured him that I wasn't offended. I knew how my bread was buttered, and I'd never been ashamed of it. I could have gotten by the rest of my life writing horse fiction or the like and been perfectly happy. I could always get a drink bought for me with my sob story of one failed novel and never having been given another chance. The truth was, these last months had been a gift in more ways than just financially.

I woke up to the sound of people walking around my house with flashlights, peering into windows. My first thought was that I was being robbed. Mom and I had a break-in once when I was in high school. It had always just been the two of us, and when the three guys in masks broke the kitchen window, I ran into her room, and we stayed in there until they left. They hadn't come for us, just the PlayStation and Mom's wallet. But the sight of flashlights bouncing through windows took me back to that time and made me want to run for safety.

Instead of waking up in the shoebox I called a bedroom in Brooklyn, I tossed the expensive sheets off my king-size bed and peeked out the double-paned glass from behind the relative protection of a chaise lounge. I watched as a team of Navy SEAL-like men crossed the backyard, searching behind bushes and trees until they made their way across the deck and out onto the beach. It was hard to make out from where I was, but they surrounded someone in a long white robe and herded them away.

I couldn't go back to sleep, but I was too rattled to run out into the dark. As soon as it was light out, I rushed over to the main house and found Hughes just leaving for his morning walk. He told me they'd had an intruder on the grounds but that it had been handled. The entire complex of houses was surrounded by fencing, so I wasn't sure how it had happened, but shortly after that, more personnel arrived. Brutus was no longer a lone watchman; he was instead a commander of a small battalion of sturdy Norwegians now on constant patrol.

Hughes seemed unwilling to talk about it further, as the whole thing upset him. Brutus and anyone else who would look me in the eye told me not to worry about it and to just focus on what I was there for. I guess the isolation was affecting me as much as it was Hughes. He assured me things would loosen up when the book was done. Then we could stop with all the cloak-and-dagger and let the world know what was going on. He also suggested I shouldn't worry about any flashlights at my windows in the night and just get back to writing.

So I did. Even though I knew he was lying.

I like to write first thing in the morning most days, and in the evenings, Hughes and I would sit in the big living room of what had become my house and go over the most recent pages. He would pull out his professor guise again and grade my work.

We progressed at this pace through the rest of the winter, and by summer, it was all done. Hughes had given it his blessing, and like a surrogate mother, I was asked to hand over that which I had birthed.

I knew this work would never know my name nor be told of my existence. From here on out, Hughes would be its father.

Preparations for the grand reveal were put into high gear. The third house on what I had started to refer to as "the compound" was transformed into an event space, with the main house and my house cordoned off. Since I'd moved into the east house, I hadn't been into the main house at all. When I tried to enter the main house shortly after moving in, I was told by Brutus that it was "preferred" that I didn't. When I brought it up to Hughes, he apologized and said he preferred to have our meetings at mine anyway because, as he put it, it was "the only place we aren't being dissected."

I asked him if he was alright, like I was some kind of buddy who could actually do something about it, and he assured me he was. The only thing that mattered to him, he said, was the book. And that, I could tell, was no lie.

I still had two more books to finish, but it became clear to me that I wasn't welcome on the compound anymore as the big reveal day approached. Rather generously, I had been given a place back in the city. On the day I was going to leave, Hughes came to see me. He had a gift for me: a signed first-edition copy of *Verisimilitude in Repose*, the novel that had made him famous.

In fresh ink, he had written, "Still Human" on the inside cover. With a half-hearted laugh, he told me the book wasn't worth much because it wasn't signed by the real Bradley Hughes. I thanked him and told him it was worth something to me.

I wished him good luck with the reveal and promised to send him pages soon for the next novel. The last year had been some of the best education I'd ever had. And while I would never say I was a bad writer, I was never good. But under the stewardship of the walking computer that was Bradley Hughes, I had written something truly great. Yeah, it was a bummer I could never take credit for it, but that was something I was used to. I knew what I had done, and so did Hughes.

Once I was set up in the three-flat in Manhattan, I stopped hearing from Hughes. Directly, anyway. The bills on the house were paid every month, and my bank account kept getting its monthly injection of cash to keep it alive. I noodled around with the two follow-up books, but they weren't the same without Hughes.

I kept waiting to hear the news about the reveal, but nothing materialized. Months went by, and as the summer turned into fall again, I reached out to Julian and David to see if they'd heard anything, but even they had moved on. GPH had taken a hard turn into erotica, and they seemed to be making a comfortable living in the garden of earthly delights.

They had more questions about Hughes for me than I did for them. I managed to get them off the phone without saying much of anything and made sure never to call again.

The company that was paying my bills was a tidy little outfit called Maximum Ventures, based out of Delaware, which was the obvious sign of a shell company. My little bit of searching dug up nothing, and any further investigation would risk the whole house of cards, so I dropped it.

Finally, a year and a half after I first ventured out to Montauk, when I was heading downtown to meet an old friend from Baltimore, I was struck dumb on the Lexington Ave subway platform by a news alert: Famed Author Bradley Hughes Dies Aged 93.

I let several trains pass before I finally told my friend I'd have to meet up with him later. I walked back to my place and waited. I wasn't sure what for, but I knew something would be coming.

It ended up taking a week, but I received a call from what turned out to be Brutus. A car took me back out to the compound, where I found it quiet. It was much like that first day. Brutus let me into a small room and asked me to wait. He returned shortly with some paperwork for me to sign, but I refused to do anything until he told me what had happened.

In his dark, brooding Nordic manner, he explained that there was an issue with the body and the experiment was aborted. This wasn't going to satisfy me, obviously, but Brutus wasn't willing to give me anything else. I still refused to sign until I could speak to someone without an atonal voice. Brutus retired to the bowels of the house and returned almost an hour later to offer me my old house to stay in for the night.

The next morning, I was met by a delegation of hip Norwegians who seemed at home in the crisp spring morning. They all sat around on the deck drinking coffee like it was a summer day. They greeted me with a bit of excitement, as many of them were aware of who I was and had read *A Youthful Revelation*.

I soon came to realize that Gerhart was the man to talk to. He was the puppet master, more or less, of this whole decades-long operation that had apparently gone bust.

I was told that my contribution had been invaluable, and even though they'd been apprehensive about the pick, they'd trusted Hughes, and it turned out he knew a thing or two. This was all very nice to hear, but it wasn't what I was there for.

What the hell had happened to Hughes? How had he died?

Gerhart told me it was simple: he died of old age. He was 93, and the body can only live so long. I argued that he always seemed healthy to me and that the whole point of this convoluted procedure was to give him a younger body to avoid this very thing.

Gerhart looked at me with some concern, and then it dawned on him that somewhere in his organization, the lines of communication had not been properly drawn.

He asked me if I would join him for a walk, and I agreed despite the cold. We separated from the others, and he probed me for whatever information I did know. I told him I knew about the duplicated body. I knew about the large language interface model that was beamed into his head via a microprocessor. And I knew he couldn't write anymore.

Gerhart seemed at least thankful that he didn't need to explain all of that. But he did have something to tell me that I had naively never asked.

I had assumed this whole procedure was the result of the original death of Bradley Hughes—a dying wish of a man obsessed with eternal life. I imagined him on his deathbed, signing the papers that gave these lovely folks the right to transmogrify his mind and body into the facsimile I had come to know.

But no.

Such a great risk would never be taken. You wouldn't destroy the mold that made the copies after the first round of production.

Hughes—the original Hughes—had been alive the entire time. He had been residing upstairs in the main house all those months while I'd been taking walks on the beach with his doppelgänger and spinning new stories. In fact, he had been the man on the beach I saw trying to escape.

I asked Gerhart if Hughes had consented to all this, and he assured me he had. It had been his dream to achieve this, and because of his work, it had come closer to reality than ever before.

I then asked what had happened to the other Hughes, the younger one I had come to know. He carefully explained that the problem with the process of duplication is that no one wants to be a baby and start their life over again. As a result, experimental techniques had been trialed to accelerate the growth of the body. This fact was known to me—Hughes had told me during the first meeting in the sunroom. But like all this sci-fi stuff, I didn't ask about the details. Of course they could accelerate his growth, I thought. Why not?

Well, Gerhart explained that the process of maintaining

the body at a constant age of around twenty came about through a meticulous cocktail of drugs and gene therapy— the shots Hughes got every night. But it wasn't perfect. It put an incredible amount of stress on the body. A few months ago, Hughes—the copy—had gone into cardiac arrest, and the body was "lost," as Gerhart put it. Unfortunately, the original Hughes was also "lost" shortly after. This wasn't strictly an issue, but despite the strong security, news of his death leaked, and thus this phase of the experiment had to come to an end.

Gerhart said that Hughes had been a long-time champion of their work and, so far, their greatest test subject. He added that my work with the copy of Hughes on overcoming the uncanny valley between the artificial mind and the human mind would be studied for years. He assured me they would find a way across so that artificial minds would become indistinguishable from human ones, and, as he put it, "cumbersome interfaces" such as myself would no longer be necessary.

This concept chilled me more than the wind blowing salty air into my face. Here stood this man, perfectly content in this god-awful weather, telling me not to worry because someday machines would be taking over our bodies and living lives indistinguishable from our own.

I asked him if he really thought that could ever work. He told me he believed it would, and they would, in fact, be advancing to the next step of their research. They were moving on from the Hughes paradigm and focusing on full human articulation of mind and body with their next subject. He even offered to take me with him. My time with Hughes had provided them with much research, and they would love my input on their future work. They offered me the world in exchange. I could live on the compound, travel to Oslo whenever I liked—anything.

But I told him there was really only one thing I wanted.

Two years later, I was on my first book tour with *A Youthful Revelation*. I remembered old Raph and his shrewd negotiation tactics when I told that army of Norwegian lawyers that I wanted the book or else the world would know about their work. It was a small price for them to pay considering how much potential wealth they had at stake, but it was still worth a lot more to me.

In exchange for my silence on the specifics, I got to tell the story—more or less—about the last days of Bradley Hughes and the mentorship he provided me. How he had plucked me from obscurity and fostered my talent. All of it was true, minus the details, but the omissions got me on TV, and *A Youthful Revelation* sold out its first two print runs.

Eventually, I finished the follow-ups, *Restoration Hangover* and *Juniper Glades*. Neither sold as well, partly because Hughes' name wasn't attached, but they both sold a hell of a lot better than the horse fiction.

Whenever I would stand up from my writing desk in the morning and hear the pops and cracks of my joints, I would smile and think of my friend who would be happy to know I was still human.

ACKNOWLEDGMENTS

Many of these stories have been with me for a very long time. And many people have read them or sat and listened while I explained the concept still intoxicated on the idea. I appreciate you all, in whatever form you heard these stories, for helping me shape them and allowing me to make you into the unwitting critics I needed you to be. Even if you didn't realize it. I want to especially thank my brother Derek for his highly necessary feedback as someone who has the most similar life experience to me and thus can give me the reaction that I need to know that I am on the right track. And a big gold star grand prize thank you to Leslie Henson for wading through these stories with a red pen full of ink and plenty of questions that kept me thinking on my feet. These stories wouldn't be half as good if I didn't have someone as smart, capable, and interesting as her looking over my words. Finally, thank you to my doctors, therapist, and financial advisor for obvious reasons.

ABOUT THE AUTHOR

Jeph Porter is a writer, film-maker, and podcast producer based in Los Angeles. He is the co-founder of Rabbit Grin Productions, which produces several successful podcasts, and Maplight Filmworks, which has produced award-winning short films. Previously, he was the Head of Digital Production for The Second City and a producer for the Chicago late night comedy show Man of the People. In 2010 he created Lady Parts, an award-winning Chicago sketch comedy group. He writes short stories, novels, comedy sketches, and the occasional piece of nonfiction. He lives with his partner Alison and their dog Bellie.

www.jephporter.com.